Anything 4 Profit

TO: DARRELL — PRECIATE THE SUPPORT HOMEY — ENJOY MY ART! AMEN

"THINK YOU REALLY KNOW ABOUT THE DIRTY SOUTH? THINK AGAIN!"

JUSTIN "AMEN" FLOYD

Published By:
Synergy Publications
P.O. Box 210-987
Brooklyn, NY 11221

www.SynergyPublications.com

Library of Congress Control Number: 2010931123

ISBN: 978-09752980-7-7

Cover Design: Oddball Dsgn

Written by: Justin "Amen" Floyd for Synergy Publications

Edited by: Caroline McGill for Synergy Publications

Dedicated to my lil' sister, Jazz

I love you "Baby Girl"… Unconditionally

Acknowledgements

I'm not supposed to be here. No hyperbole, no exaggeration, no bullshit. I'm not supposed to be here, releasing my first book (written during some of my deepest, darkest, most depressing days in the depths of solitude). I'm supposed to be dead, in prison serving a life sentence without the possibility of parole, or on Death Row. ...But I'm not. That being said I've got to give thanks to a God that saw the best in me when I was at my absolute wretched worst. I don't believe in any particular religion, but I do believe in God, and in myself.

On this tumultuous journey called life, there have been very few people that have been there from the beginning, and left a lasting impression on my heart. I want to take this time to acknowledge those people, and say thanks for being there when I was at the bottom of the bottom. Through the early years of my development, these were the people who shaped my young mind. Later on, as incarceration became the norm in my life, these were the people who held me down and helped me maintain my sanity in an insane reality.

First, I wanna say thank-you to my mama, Kirby, for carrying me in her womb for nine months. Next I'd like to say thank-you to my Aunt Rose for cultivating that revolutionary spirit within me, and for giving me a sense of Black Pride (I guess making me watch Shaka Zulu all those times actually paid off! LOL). Thanks to my cousin Neal who was like an older brother to me when I was younger, and introduced me to REAL Hip-Hop (I used to kill you on that Nintendo though, nigga!). Much love goes out to my baby sister Jazzmin Justine Farmer. I love you "baby girl". Your letters gave me the strength and a reason to keep going when I really didn't want to. Thick or thin, I got you lil' sis!! My cousin Lisa for all of the real advice and encouraging words over the years. Also my brother Kevin, and my older sister Kirich.

Outside of my immediate family, I wanna give a shout out to the numerous people who've shown their love, support, and shared their knowledge with a young brother who was beyond out of control, and on a path of self destruction. Your words were not in vain. It just took me a little minute to comprehend the meaning... Shout out to all the REAL niggas (NOT the rapists, child molesters. or snitches!!) locked down in the various institutions across Amerikkka! Especially those brothers who strengthened their minds and became politically conscious during their bids. Your consciousness about who you are, and where you come from makes you a threat to the establishment. Therefore you are no longer an inmate, you are now a political prisoner in an ongoing war to liberate the minds of others who are trapped in the triple stages of darkness: deaf, dumb and blind. Salute! Shout out to all the REAL niggas doing bids throughout the South Carolina Department of Corruption!! Lee County C.I., Evans C.I., Perry C.I., Ridgeland C.I., Tyger River... The list goes on. Just know that I've been exactly where you're at, and I made it... Sky's the limit, my niggas!!

A special shout out goes to my publisher, my friend, my homey, my big "sister" Caroline McGill. Over the months that we've known each other you've truly been there when I needed you, and gave me an opportunity to make my dream a reality. And for that I will forever be grateful. We finna take this book game OVER!! And much love to the whole McGill family for showing genuine love whenever I come through. Shout out to all the street book vendors who've shown support for my work. One of the first being Chris the

BK Bookman out there on Pitkin Ave. What it is, nigga? I told you it was finna happen, homey!!

Last but certainly not least, I wanna give a big shout out to my many, many detractors, enemies, and just overall naysayers. All of those coward ass people who failed to pursue their own dreams, and therefore told me I shouldn't, wouldn't, or couldn't pursue mine. I just wanna say this... I'm here!!! And I ain't stopping. Matter fact I'm just getting started! May my success be the Ether that eats away at your envious souls every time you hear my name mentioned, or see my book. I guess what they say is true: the last laugh truly is the loudest!!! And right now I'm LMMAO!

P.S. - Much love to my homegirl Drienna McMillan Sloan, and her company Envy Entertainment for holdin' a brother down back home. GREENVILLE, S.C. STAND UP!

The Introduction

BOOM! BOOM! BOOM! The hail of shots fired from the .44 caliber cannon pierced the silence of the hot, humid summer night. It was dark, but for brief seconds, the flash from the muzzle of the gun illuminated the horrific scene taking place. A body dropped to the ground, and two figures dressed in black from head to toe fled as fast as their legs would carry them.

Left behind on the asphalt was another lifeless body of a young, Black man. He was lying face down in a pool of blood, so his white Nike Air Force Ones slowly turned crimson. His new Coogi jeans were now filled with the stench of piss and shit. And his face was so badly disfigured from the gunshot wounds that if not for his teeth, his body would have remained unidentified. Needless to say, at his funeral the casket would remain closed.

This is the story of three friends from the bottom, born into poverty, pain, and despair. Those same conditions plague Blacks like a disease in inner-city neighborhoods. And they are especially severe in the racially oppressive atmosphere of the Deep South.

Backs to the wall, and tired of being pawns in the White man's proverbial chess game, the friends made a vow amongst themselves to get money…by any mothafuckin' means possible! Murder, robbery, extortion, kidnapping, or fraud. They would do anything for profit. And any opposition to their goals was met with savage

8

violence. Only those also raised in the gutter would understand or relate to their mentality. Either you rolled with them, or you got rolled the fuck over. It was real simple. No mercy, no remorse.

Like I said, this is the story of three friends, and their struggle to rise above the squalid socio-economic conditions they were born into. Me? My name is AMEN. I'm just the vessel being used to bring this story to you. Letting you see life through their eyes. Come take a glimpse into their world. A place where the rules and morals of American society cease to have any meaning. To understand these characters, you have to first see how they came about...

Greenville, S.C. - Summer of '85

"PUSH, PUSH!" The doctor yelled at the young girl lying on the bed in the delivery room of St. Francis Hospital. "Come on Tracy, he's almost out. I can see the head! Push, Tracy!"

"I can't Dr. Smith, I can't, I can't... I'm just so tired," said Tracy exhaustedly.

"Tracy, listen. Give me one more good push, okay?"

Tracy pushed with all the strength she had remaining in her young, frail, weakened body, and out came a brown, wrinkled baby boy, crying and screaming at the top of his lungs. It was like he was protesting the fact that he was forced into such a cold, callous world.

"It's a boy, Tracy, it's a boy," Dr. Smith stated as he clipped the umbilical cord. The nurse cleaned the baby off, wrapped him in a light blue blanket, and then handed the bawling infant over to his mother. As she stared at the life she had just brought into the world, the smile on Tracy's face illuminated the entire delivery room.

"What are you going to name him?" asked the nurse on call, as she gently took the baby back.

Tracy was totally exhausted from being in labor for more than 18 hours. She whispered, "Michael. His name is Michael." She named the newborn baby after the man whom she had naively given her virginity and her young heart to. The man who had gotten her pregnant. The man who had said he loved her. The man who had said he would die for her. The same man had deserted her the moment she told him that she was pregnant with his child. And yet her heart still ached at the mere thought of him.

"Doctor, Doctor!" yelled the nurse. "She's hemorrhaging! Losing too much blood here! She's going into cardiac arrest! We're losing her!"

"Code Red! Code Red, we've got a code red in Delivery Room #2!" yelled Dr. Smith. "All available medical personnel report to Delivery Room number 2 stat!!" the voice blared out over the intercom.

Delivery room #2 filled with nurses and doctors, all attempting to revive the young woman who lay dying on the hospital bed, bleeding to death. But their heroic efforts were in vain. At the tender age of 16, Tracy Denise Dillinger was dead.

Her parents, who had been sitting in the waiting room throughout the entire ordeal, broke down and burst into tears when the doctor came out and delivered the heartbreaking news that their only child—their baby girl, had died while giving birth to a son that was fatherless… a bastard.

Unable to deal with the constant reminder of their teenage daughter's sexual carelessness and subsequent death, her parents looked into the nursery at their grandson for the first and last time. After talking it over, they made the decision to put the child up for adoption.

So on the same day the world gained a new life, two were also lost. One lost to the grave, the other to the system. The date was June 16th 1985, and that was how Mike came into the world. All alone.

Greenville, S.C. - Summer of '85

The crack epidemic grew out of control during the Reagan Administration. It had already begun to devour the impoverished inhabitants of the ghettos of most major cities in America, but it had yet to reach smaller cities in the south like Greenville, S.C. So fiends were still freebasing their coke in glass pipes, aluminum cans, or whatever other object that could stand the intense heat of the fire used to turn the coke into smoke, so they could inhale it and get a blast. Smoking the cocaine instead of snorting it up their noses gave them a more intense high.

The acrid smell of freebase smoke filled the air of a house, which was really nothing more than an old boarded up shack where smokers and fiends got high. A strong gust of wind could've probably blown that shit down like a piece of cardboard. Outside in the front yard, there were several old beat up Chevy's and Fords, whose best years were long behind them. The unkempt grass and weeds were slowly devouring their rusty remains.

Inside, there were several base-heads indulging in their habit. Most notably was a young woman by the name of Gloria Davis, affectionately called Glo by her friends and family. Gloria was the epitome of the word sexy. She had size 36 D breasts, a 22 inch waist, and an onion cut to make grown men cry. With a caramel complexion and big, brown, bedroom eyes, Gloria was what men in her day would consider a "Brick-House" like that Commodores song.

But Gloria had a habit. And she would stop at nothing to support it. Over the years she'd been using, Gloria had quickly slipped and hit rock bottom. She had done everything from sell her furniture, to sell her body to get high.

"Mmmmm, Gloria, there it is, baby! Suck that dick, girl. Yeah baby, just like that, just like that! Damn Gloria, you give the best head in the fuckin' world, gurl."

Gloria was on her knees with some random dude's penis in her mouth, sucking on it as if her life depended on it. And in a sense it did. She needed that trick to get high. That's all she lived for. With one hand working the strangers' shaft, and the other gripping the cheap dresser for balance, she worked her head back and forth like a pro, humming and slobbering all over his dick until he released his hot seed into her mouth. Gloria pretended to swallow, and licked her lips. In her sexiest voice, she said, "Damn baby, yo' milk sho' taste good."

The stranger laughed, and gathered his clothes and got dressed. He left a small bag of white powder on the dresser as payment for the excellent service he had just received, and was on his way.

As soon as the trick left, Gloria spit his thick semen onto the floor and wiped her mouth with the back of her hand. For a brief second, she wondered what she had become. She thought of the way she had been raised. She was from a pretty decent home.

Any reasoning in her mind was quickly overpowered by her urge to get high. She hurried over to the bag of white the trick had left on the table and fiendishly grabbed at the bag. She tore it open and placed the contents inside an empty aluminum can she had nearby. She grabbed her lighter off the dresser, and put flame to the can until the coke turned to thick smoke, and then she took a good hit. The blissful effect was almost immediate. Gloria closed her eyes and enjoyed the feeling. The drug provided her with an escape. She had a lot of demons, and they haunted her when she wasn't high.

She was sitting there in a drug induced haze when two men entered the small room. In the room, there was nothing more than an old dresser and a filthy mattress, soiled from numerous men's semen, sweat, and other bodily fluids. The two men began to aggressively fondle Gloria, grabbing at her firm ass and tits. One of them leered at her, and said, "You gon' let us get some of that good pussy, gurl? Huh?"

Glo was nervous, but the crack whore in her said, "How much y'all gon' pay me?"

"Bitch, fuck that," the shorter one slurred, with the scent of liquor loud on his breath. He pulled out a 6 inch blade, and said, "This one's gon' be on the house." He then grabbed Gloria by the neck, and threw her down on the dirty mattress.

"You know what time it is," said the taller, lighter skinned hound. "Either you gon' fuck, or you gon' die. It's yo' choice, bitch. What's up?"

Filled with fear, Gloria closed her eyes, opened her legs, and let the men have their way with her. They violated her young body every way they knew how. One of them choked her hard as hell while he pounded her, until she blacked out.

When she finally opened her eyes, the men were gone. They left her lying in a pool of sticky semen and blood. She gathered what little strength she had left, and attempted to walk to the bathroom. Disoriented and weak, she staggered down the hallway. Before she could reach there, her legs gave out and her mind went blank again. Gloria fell to the dirty, hard and splintered wooden floor. She lay there naked and unconscious for hours.

Nine months later, Gloria gave birth to twins. They were a little underweight because she had continued getting high throughout her pregnancy, but they were beautiful. She named the girl Tameka, and the boy she named Anthony. When asked who their father was, Gloria hung her head in shame. The nurse didn't see the silent tears she shed. The date was March 9th, 1986. That was how Meka and Ant-D got here.

Fast forward twenty years...

Chapter 1

The Ville... August, 2006

A woman's voice came blaring from a cheap television that was bolted down to a dilapidated nightstand. "*Tonight on the Fox 10 O'clock news... Police have found an unidentified body brutally murdered in the Kennedy Park section of Greenville. The body has suffered numerous gunshot wounds to the face and chest areas. Authorities believe that this murder was the result of a drug transaction gone bad. If you have any information pertaining to this crime, please call 1-800-crimestoppers, or the Greenville county sheriff's office. More details to follow...*"

"A yo' Ant, did you see that nigga's muh'fuckin' face when I pulled the pistol on his monkey ass, my nigga!?" asked Mike animatedly. He and Ant sat in a low-budget motel room, reliving the murderous events that they were responsible for. They had committed the crimes just hours earlier.

"Man, that nigga's eyes got bigger than a deer's caught in the headlights of an 18 wheeler!" laughed Ant D.

"But do you think he shit on his self befo', or after I peeled his shit back?" asked Mike jokingly.

"Probably befo', dog. Er'body know Tremone was more pussy than four dykes havin' an orgy. I'm surprised that old Sideshow

Bob, Homey the Clown ass nigga was even out here tryna hustle, dog."

"You ain't even bullshittin'. That was the easiest, quickest 30 G's I ever done made in my fuckin' life, my nigga."

"Damn right," Ant D said. "Thirty for you, thirty for me."

"Man, look here, over the past few months we done licked muh'fuckas for 'bout 250 grand…"

"At least!" yelled Ant D.

"That's my whole point though, my nigga. We just blowin' that shit, homey. We ain't doin' shit wit' it. We robbin' muh'fuckas, killin' niggas, riskin' doin' a fuckin' bid, and then we just blow that shit, and do it again! Man, we gotta slow down, and start tryna make this money do gymnastics for *us*! We gotta get it, then figure out how we gon' wash it without them boys gettin' on our ass. I ain't tryna go in and do no mo' time. You know them alphabet boys like flies on shit once they figure they got a case."

"Maaaaaan, don't even stress that shit. I'm already on it," said Ant D. "You remember my Uncle Bug, right?"

"Yeah," Mike chuckled. "I remember that ugly ass mothafucka'. Man, they gave that nigga the right name too. Dude look like a fuckin bug for real! Big, black, ugly ass muh'fucka! I know he be paying for pussy, 'cause I swear, that's 'bout the only way he gon' get his dick wet…except fo' when he wash. And shiiiiiit, the way that nigga be smellin', I ain't even sho' he do that," Mike said, cracking up.

"Yeah, yeah, yeah. But all bullshit aside tho', peep game, Mike. He was tellin' me 'bout this building that's on sale in the Burg for 'bout 400 G's. He said it used to be a storage facility, but that shit shut down. All we gotta do is buy it, fix it up, and open up our own shit. You always talkin' 'bout having your own strip club and shit, right? Well this the spot, my nigga. Now yo' ass can stop talkin' 'bout it, and start being 'bout it and make that shit happen. We can put our paper through the fuckin' cleaners, and at the same time, have the baddest bitches in the south workin' at our club!" said Ant

D enthusiastically. "Nigga, we'll be the youngest, flyest niggas in the Upstate with our own spot… gettin' it!!" he yelled excitedly.

"That sound like a muh'fuckin' plan," Mike stated. "But as of right now, we only got 'bout 100 saved up to play with. We gon' need at least a good 8 or 900 to make that shit pop like its 'posed to. So you know what that means."

"Mo' money, Mo' murder," they said in unison. The two trigger happy pals both laughed. They were young, fearless, and foolish, so they both thought they were invincible.

"Ant D, go 'head and stop bullshittin'. Roll up some of that sticky we got from Trap," Mike said passing Ant D a clear plastic baggy filled with big buds of purple haze.

"Yeah, I better roll this shit, 'cause I swear, yo' non-rollin' ass will have that shit fallin' apart. Weed fallin' all out the blunt, and all type of shit!" Ant D took a bud out, broke it down, and rolled a blunt that looked like it was about 9 months pregnant. He grabbed a lighter off the dresser, lit the blunt, and took a deep pull, savoring the way the smoke filled his lungs.

"Take two and pass, nigga. You already know what it is," said Mike.

Ant D passed the blunt to Mike, already beginning to feel a little buzz from the potent, exotic marijuana they were smoking. The pungent aroma of the "exotic" permeated the small motel room they were in. To avoid some nosey ass, potential do-gooder walking by and smelling the smoke, and possibly calling the law, Mike got a towel from the bathroom. He wet it, and placed it at the crack of the bottom of the door. That would help keep the smell from escaping. That was a little trick he had learned during one of his numerous stints in The Department of Juvenile Justice.

The Camelot, the motel they were holed up in counting their blood money, was nothing but a hole in a wall. It was owned by some immigrant Indians who were exploiting the poor economic conditions that black people were plagued with in the south, getting rich off their sweat and blood. "The Lot" was where the hoes came to get fucked, and the heads came to get high. Dope boys went there to trap, and the jack boys came to catch a lick.

So when they heard a woman outside screaming at the top of her lungs for the police, Mike and Ant D looked at each other. They were thinking the same thing. It was time to get the fuck outta Dodge!

"Let's get light, Ant D. Ain't no point tryna explain to the police what we doin' in here with 60 stacks of cash money."

"Shiiiiiiiiiiiiit, I was thinkin' the same thang, my nigga."

They both grabbed what few belongings they had, and hurried outside to Mike's candy painted, money green, box Chevy Caprice. It was sitting high on 26 inch chrome Giovanna rims, wrapped in low profile Pirelli tires. Mike started the car up and put some old shit from Tip's "Urban Legend" album on blast.

"*Ride wit me nigga, let me show you where we kick it at - Where hustlers get them chickens at and T.i.p be chillin at...*"

As Mike was pulling out of the parking lot he looked in the rearview mirror, only to see the blue lights of a Greenville County police car flashing behind them, signaling for him to pull over.

Without even so much as a second thought, Mike slammed his foot down on the accelerator. The Pirelli tires screamed and left a trail of burnt rubber on the asphalt. Ant D, who had been in the passenger seat bobbing his head along to the beat, was forcefully thrown back in his seat. The Chevy propelled down the road, and the chase was on.

"What the fuck..." Before Ant D could finish his statement, Mike ran a series of red lights, and swerved onto a side road. The dark blue police cruiser followed close behind, with its sirens blaring.

"Man, these pussy muh'fuckas is on our ass," yelled Mike. He gripped the steering wheel and sped through the night, attempting to shake the county car behind them.

"Damn! Boy, I swear to God I ain't tryna see that county tonight, nigga! I can't go to jail, my mama cookin' chicken for dinner," Ant joked. But at the same time, he was as serious as cancer. He looked in the rearview mirror.

"Nigga, I got this here." Mike laughed, temporarily taking his eyes off the road.

"Oooooooh shit!!! Nigga, watch out!" Ant was scared to death, his hands fiercely gripping the dashboard.

Mike turned his attention back to the road, and swerved to the right just in time to avoid a head on collision with an oncoming car in the other lane. He said, "Damn, that was close! Nigga, it sounded like you was 'bout to shit on yo'self." He was fucking with Ant. That was a close brush with death, so nervous beads of sweat had started to form on his forehead too.

"Nigga, fuck you! Just drive this muh'fucka!"

By now they had reached speeds in excess of 70 mph. And on those small unpaved back roads, one wrong move could be fatal. "Goddamn, this muh'fucka is still on our ass!" said Mike, as he continued to swerve recklessly in and out of lanes. He was hoping that the cop would lose heart, and give up on the chase. But no such luck.

"Mike, look here. Just get us to that lil' cut over there by Lakeside Park, and we'll jump out and split-up on his monkey ass. Then we can meet up at Neesy's house over there in Rockvale. Ain't no way that cracker gon' be able to catch us, good as we know them woods over there."

"Yeah, but that mean I gotta leave my Chevy behind." There was a hint of sadness in Mike's voice. He steered the car onto the wrong side of the street, hoping to scare the pig off like that. But once again, no such luck.

Mike continued debating. "Which means they gonna know it was me and you, 'cause this shit registered in my name. Plus our prints is all over this bitch."

"Look here, nigga. You tryna be sittin' up in the muh'fuckin' county tonight, in one of them pissy ass, packed ass holding cells with a bunch of drunks and crack heads all night? Waiting to see a judge to make bail? I know I ain't!"

Mike had to think fast. His Chevy was his baby, but an O.G. named Big Rick, who was now on Death Row withering away, had put him up on game a long time ago. Once you embraced the streets, you could never become attached to anything that you couldn't walk away from in 30 seconds or less. *"Young blood, sometimes 30 seconds can be all the time you got between death, a life sentence, or living to see another day."*

With that thought in mind, Mike swerved recklessly onto the road that would take them in the direction of the park. He was driving so fast and so reckless, he nearly wrecked and flipped the car over about four times. And Greenville County's "finest" still refused to stop the chase.

"Ok nigga, we almost there! As soon as we get to the cut, you already know what it is," said Mike frantically.

"Fa' sho'. We hop out, toss the guns, and split up and hit the woods 'til we lose this clown. Then we meet up at Neesy's house."

Suddenly, Mike made a hard right onto a dirt road, and killed his lights. The Chevy almost spun out of control, and a huge cloud of dirt went up into the air. The dark road was illuminated only by the dim glimmer of the moon. That road led into the woods that were part of Lakeside Park. At the end of the road, there was a small opening that led into the woods. Right on the other side of the woods was a 'hood called Rockvale, where one of Ant's numerous girlfriends, Neesy, shared a house with her sister and her kids.

As Mike approached the woods, he attempted to pump the brakes but the dirt road made it difficult to maintain control of the car, let alone slow down. The forest raced towards them, and he slammed his foot down on the brake. The car skidded forward until it collided with a tree at the beginning of the path. The impact was bad, but not bad enough to prevent Mike and Ant from jumping out. They grabbed their money and cell phones, and ran into the woods like two runaway slaves.

The officer who had initiated the high speed chase tried to bring his car to an abrupt stop, but he ended up colliding into the back of Mike's car. He was dazed for a second, but he jumped out and ran into the woods with his gun drawn, and flashlight out. "Greenville County Sheriff's Department! Stop!"

He might as well have been talking to one of the trees because Ant D and Mike were ghost.

Within seconds, there were several Greenville County police cars at the scene, with their spotlights on, and their blue lights flashing. The K-9 unit was dispatched, and there was also a police helicopter circling overhead like a vulture waiting to swoop down and pick off its prey.

But it was all for nothing. Ant D and Mike had escaped the long arm of the law. At least for the moment.

Chapter 2

Inside a plush, luxurious bedroom, located in a mini mansion in Easley, South Carolina, two lovers were sexually devouring each other on top of red satin sheets that covered a King sized, four post bed.

"Damn, Meka! I'm 'bout to bust, baby. Damn girl, I swear yo' pussy is so fuckin' *good*!"

"Go 'head and bust that nut in this pussy, daddy. Beat it up for me, daddy," Meka moaned.

Twan was on top of Meka, banging away at her insides and trying to make her feel it up in her throat. The sound of their hot sweaty bodies banging together filled the room, along with the aroma of their sex.

Meka held her legs up in the air as wide as possible, and started moaning, "Fuck me, daddy, fuck me hard, daddy. I'm your little slut, baby." While talking dirty, she made the sexiest faces she could.

Right before Twan was about to cum, he pulled his dick out of Meka's pussy and blasted his hot, sticky semen all over her stomach. Meka wiped his cum up with her hand, and made sure he saw her lick every drop off her palm and fingers.

Exhausted, Twan rolled off of Meka and lay on his side facing her. "Meka, you know I love you, right?" asked Twan.

"Yeah, I know that, daddy. I know. I love you too." She gave him the warmest, sincerest smile, and made Twan blush. Meka was good.

After that, she said, "Look, baby. I gotta go wash up, and get dressed. I got some things I need to do today." She got up and stretched.

"Come on and get yo' ass back in bed, Meka," Twan said, attempting to grab her hand. "Spend the weekend with me."

"I will, Twan, but first I gotta go home and check on some things. I'll be back later."

Meka went into the bathroom to take a shower. Before she got in, she stood in front of the full length mirror and admired her honey brown body. She was so bad she had the ability to make niggas act the fool. At 5'5", 135 pounds, Meka was the epitome of the word "thick." She had baby doll eyes, and full sensuous lips that men loved seeing her lick. Her waist was small, and her breasts were full, with large brown nipples. Her ass was large and juicy, and it jiggled whenever she walked. Thick, toned thighs and legs that were slightly bowed were the icing on top of the mouth-watering cake.

Meka liked to pamper herself, so every week she got her hair done, and hit up the nail salon for a fresh manni/peddi. And usually at the expense of some sucker who hadn't even fucked her yet. Meka was a dime. Naw, fuck that, Meka was a quarter! All the old heads said she was the spitting image of her mama, Glo, before she started smoking that shit.

Still admiring her body, Meka rubbed her nipples with one hand, and her still wet, throbbing pussy with the other. "Damn, let me stop and get my ass in the shower," she whispered to herself.

After showering, Meka went and got her clothes out of her overnight bag, and got dressed. She put on some skin tight Apple Bottoms that accentuated her ass, and a light blue blouse that showed off her cleavage. The flat, gold gladiator sandals she put on exposed her sexy pedicured toes. Glancing at her watch, she saw that it was already after 12 'noon that Saturday.

She kissed Twan goodbye, and stepped outside into the bright sunlight of the day. She walked over to her Chrysler 300c, hopped in, and sped away. She was headed toward District 25. That was the 'hood she was from.

$$$

"Goddamn, Ant D, where the fuck is yo' crazy ass sister at? Man, ever since we been kids, her ass be late for shit," said Mike.

It had been a few days since Ant D and Mike's last lick, and their close encounter with the law. They had laid low for a couple of days, so they were thirsty. The partners yearned another opportunity to showcase their fundraising skills, so they were both anxious to hear the information they hoped Meka had obtained.

Ant shook his head, and said, "Ain't no tellin', dog. But she'll pop up in a minute."

"Ant, Mike, y'all hungry? Y'all want something to eat?" asked Gloria, from the kitchen door.

"What you cookin' on, mama?"

"Some fried chicken," Gloria responded.

"Damn right," said Ant D.

Mike rubbed his hands together, and said, "Yeah, Ms. D, let me get some of that too. Don't *nobody* in the south fry that barnyard pimp like you!"

Gloria headed in the kitchen, and began to bread the chicken with her own secret blend of flour and an assortment of spices that gave her chicken its own special flavor. Then she dropped each piece into a deep fryer that was filled with hot grease.

At about 12:40 P.M. Meka walked through the back door and smelled the aroma of the fried chicken Gloria was in the kitchen whipping up.

"Damn, mama, you got this house smellin' good!" exclaimed Meka.

"Hey, baby. Your brother and Mike are in the living room. I'll bring the food out in a second. Soon as I get through."

"Alright, mama." Meka walked into the living room and sat down on the black leather couch across from her twin brother, and crossed her thick legs.

"Where the fuck you been at girl!?" asked Ant D, jumping up from the chair he was sitting in. "I told yo' ass to be here at 12!"

"Look, nigga, sit yo' ass the fuck down. How many times I gotta tell yo' fuckin' ass that you my brother, and *not* my fuckin' daddy. Okay? Hey Mike."

"What's poppin, Meka? I see yo' ass still can't get nowhere on time," said Mike, chuckling.

"You know what? Fuck *both* y'all niggas," Meka replied.

"Alright, alright, let's kill the bullshit, and get down to business," Ant D said, sitting back down in the plush leather recliner. "Did you finally find out where that nigga Twan got his shit at?"

"Yeah," replied Meka. "It took me a lil' minute, but he finally broke down and showed me the safe. It's in his bedroom closet."

"Damn… stupid ass niggas still keeping safes in their closet? Muh'fuckas must think this shit is a fuckin' movie, or one of them fairytale ass street books they livin' in, or something," Mike said incredulously. "And how the fuck did you get him to show you that anyway?" inquired Mike.

"Just the best pussy that clown ass nigga ever got in his life! This thang I got between my legs is straight crack, nigga. No Arm and Hammer, no cut, nigga. Straight drop! One hit, and you hooked," Meka said, giggling.

"When you gon' let me get a lil' sample then?" joked Mike.

"In your fuckin' dreams," Meka retorted. She knew he was only playing though. They'd been through so much shit over the years, Mike was truly like a real brother to her.

Just then, Glo walked into the living room, interrupting their criminal conversation. She was carrying a bowl full of chicken, with three sheets of paper towel at the bottom to catch the grease. She had also made some potato salad, which she carried in another bowl in her other hand. She sat the food down on the table, along with some paper plates, and everyone began to eat. Their conversation was momentarily forgotten. You knew the food was good when nobody was saying shit! Glo went back into the kitchen, and she re-emerged with three glasses, and a pitcher of grape Kool-Aid that was sweet enough to put a diabetic in a coma.

"Damn. Ms. D, we gon have to get you your own restaurant when we get this paper right. This shit here… is blazin'!" said Mike, smacking his lips.

"For real, mama," Ant D and Meka said together, as they continued stuffing their faces.

Glo took pleasure in the fact that they liked her food so much. It really made her feel good to see that they enjoyed her cooking. But what warmed her heart the most was to see her kids together, after all the craziness they had all been through over the years.

After many, many years of prostitution, degradation, and addiction, Gloria was finally clean. She had her pride and self esteem back, but more importantly she had a relationship with her kids. Mike had been in the family so long, she considered him one of hers too. Of course with all the bullshit she'd put her kids through over the years, their relationship was far from perfect. But it was still a relationship.

There wasn't a day that went by that Gloria didn't regret many of the decisions she had made over the years, selfishly chasing the next high. Maybe if she'd been a better mother, her children would've had a better life. Maybe they wouldn't be involved in the streets so heavily now. Maybe… Life was full of maybes.

She knew that her kids were knee-deep in the streets, and she knew what that type of lifestyle entailed. But Glo never tried to preach to them. She just dropped game and gave advice, whenever she could, based on her own life experiences. All that was left to do after that was get on her knees and pray to God that He'd keep her children safe.

That was ironic because for a long time, Gloria had seriously doubted the existence of God. She went through a lot when she was out there, so she'd felt like God wouldn't have allowed her to suffer that way.

Gloria had been involved in countless near-death situations. She had literally been to hell and back. But she conquered her demons and survived, so she knew there had to be a higher power. That's why she prayed for her children. She knew God was real. She was a living testimony.

She smiled at her kids again, and told them, "I'm 'bout to go and take me a lil' nap, y'all. Put them dirty dishes in the sink, and them plates in the trash when y'all get through, hear?"

"Ok mama," replied Meka. "I'll get 'em."

Mike finished off the last piece of chicken, licked his lips, and wiped his hands and mouth with a paper towel. After he burped, and excused himself, he said, "Now back to this nigga Twan."

"Yeah, how much money you think he holdin' in that safe?" Ant D asked his sister, still chewing on a mouthful of chicken and potato salad.

"I don't know fa' sho'. But it can't be no less than 4 or 500 grand with the type of weight he be movin'. He probably got some work in there too. And do you gotta talk with yo' mouth full? That shit is disgusting," Meka said, teasing her brother.

Ant opened his mouth so Meka could get a good look at the food he hadn't finished chewing on.

She made a face, and then punched him in the arm. He opened his mouth to gross his other half out again, and they both laughed.

Ant said, "Shut up, Meka, and pay close attention to what I'm finna say, 'cause it's going down. Here's the plan…"

Chapter 3

Later on that night, Meka dialed Twan's home phone number on her purple Motorola Razr. That cell phone was Meka's favorite color.

Twan answered on the 3rd ring. "Hello?"

"Hey daddy, it's me," said Meka, using her sweetest, most innocent voice.

"Damn babygirl, where you at? I thought you was gonna come back through, and spend the weekend wit' me."

"Yeah daddy, I am. But you know I had to check up on my mama, and make sure everything was alright with her."

"So, is everything cool?" Twan asked.

In a voice dripping with lust, she said, "Yeah, everything's good. But I was thinking, boo. Instead of me driving all the way back to your house in Easley, how 'bout you come into the city, and pick me up at my mama's house? That way we can go out to eat dinner at my favorite spot. Then after dinner, we can head back to your house. And then I can give you some dessert."

"And what's for dessert?" asked Twan.

"Your favorite," replied Meka. "Me... with some whipped cream, chocolate syrup, and a cherry to top it all off. You think you can handle all that, daddy?" she teased.

"Ain't nuttin' but one way to find out. I'll be there to get you in 'bout an hour, alright?"

"Okay, daddy." Meka pushed the end button on her cell phone.

"What's the word, Meka?" asked Ant D, who was standing beside her the whole time she was on the phone.

"Nigga, as close as yo' ass was, all up on me, I know damn well you ain't miss a word that nigga said," stated Meka sarcastically. "Anyway," she said, rolling her eyes. "He'll be here in about an hour to pick me up, so y'all niggas need to go 'head and get right. I'll keep him at the restaurant for a lil' minute, then take him back to his house, and do what I do."

"That's what's happenin'," said Mike. "Just make sure that nigga is exhausted by the time we get there."

"Believe me, Mike, that won't be a problem. I'ma fuck that nigga 'til he in a coma!"

"Naw, naw, we don't need him in no coma, Meka," Ant D said, grinning. "If he can't talk, then how the fuck we gon' get the safe combination outta his ass?" All three of them burst out laughing.

$$$

Fresh out of the shower, Twan started getting dressed. His mind was occupied with thoughts of Meka. That was his baby. She meant a lot to him. He had yet to meet a girl that could hold his attention and keep him captivated the way she did. With the type of money he was making, he had the baddest women the south had to offer at his fingertips. But none of them understood him like Meka did.

Thoughts of marriage crept through his head while he got fresh, throwing on a cream linen suit, and some brown leather Gucci hard bottoms.

Though Twan wasn't sitting on kingpin status just yet, he was definitely a major figure. He was part of one of The Upstate's biggest drug organizations, and was moving about ten keys a week. His uncle ran the organization, and it was he who had put him on. His uncle told him he saw the potential in him early on, so he was grooming him to take his place someday.

Twan wasn't a kingpin yet but he had no qualms with spending money like one. His philosophy was that you only lived once, so a nigga might as well live like tomorrow would never come. And the type of lifestyle Twan was engaged in, that was always a possibility. He was only a year in the game, but at twenty-four years old, he already owned his own 4 bedroom, 3 1/2 bathroom house, with a swimming pool, and large back yard. His estate was complete with a 3 car garage where he kept his black Range Rover, white 645 BMW coupe with Lamborghini doors, and an old school Chevy he had restored with his own bare hands in his spare time. He had everything he wanted. So now, with a girl who was wifey material by his side, he was already seriously considering getting out of the game. After he touched a few more millions, that is.

Despite his intelligence, and his uncle's constant advice not to get involved in a serious relationship with anything but the game, Twan couldn't help the way he felt about Meka. He had so much respect for her he never discussed his business with her. He knew she knew he was a dope boy, but he did his best to shield her from his criminal lifestyle. They'd been together for months, and he still hadn't introduced her to any of his close friends or family. Almost all of them were involved in the dope game, in some way or another.

Twan understood the crabs in a bucket, animalistic mentality of the 'hood all too well, so he didn't want Meka to wind up getting kidnapped or something. He was stacking chips like Pringles, and he knew he had become prey for the predators the second he started. In the 'hood it was simple: Survival of the fittest. The theorist Charles Darwin called it Natural Selection. So Twan took proper precautions. He had security cameras installed strategically outside his house, and a stash box in each of his vehicles for his assortment of guns and ammunition.

Before leaving his house, Twan activated the security system, and looked at the monitors in his den to make sure shit was in order. This had become a habit every time he stepped out. It was part of his routine now, since his finances had increased so drastically.

Reassured of his safety, Twan walked over to his garage and tried to decide which car to pull out. Since it was August, and the night was hot, he figured he'd take the Beemer coupe, and let the top down. Meka loved being seen in the 645. She told him that she got wet whenever she rode in it, so the 6 was a no brainer. He opened the door, got in, and started up the car. Twan was in a good mood, so he decided to blast that old school Jigga and Jermaine Dupri, "Money Ain't a Thing."

"In the Ferrari or Jaguar switchin' 4 lanes - Top down screamin' out money ain't a thing. Bubble hard in the double R flashin' the rings - With the window cracked, holla back, money ain't a thing..."

Twan rapped along with Hov', and pulled out of his garage. He was on his way to pick up his baby from her mama's house in The District.

$$$

Meka took a quick shower, and quickly dried off. She got out, and slowly and sensually rubbed Burberry lotion all over her body. Next, she walked over to her closet and tried to figure out what to wear that night. She knew she wouldn't be wearing whatever it was long, but Meka still wanted to be as fly as possible. After so many years of extreme poverty, her psyche wouldn't allow her to step out of the house looking anything less than her best. She even made shit like going to the grocery store a red carpet event.

She finally decided on a slinky black Prada dress. Twan had dropped a couple of stacks on that dress for her a few months back. It was one-shouldered, and accentuated her best assets. To add a splash of color and set the dress off, she selected a pair off metallic gold, opened toed Jimmy Choos. They were five inch stilettos, with straps up to her mid-calf. She sat down and put on her shoes first. Afterwards, not bothering to put on any underwear, she slipped into her dress.

"Meka, there's somebody at the door for you," hollered Glo

from the living room.

Meka glanced at her diamond encrusted Cartier watch, which was another gift from Twan, and saw that it was nine o'clock.

"Ok mama, I'm comin'!" yelled Meka. She sprayed herself with expensive, exotic scented perfume, and headed for the living room. When she stepped out there and saw Twan's face, immediately she knew she had made the right wardrobe decision.

"Damn, girl! You lookin' sexy as hell!" exclaimed Twan.

"Thank you, daddy. I wanted our time together this weekend to be unforgettable," said Meka, with a sly little smile on her face.

"Come here, girl. Let me get a taste of them lips real quick."

Meka walked over to Twan, and hugged his 6 foot 2 inched frame. He bent down and slipped his tongue in her mouth, and sucked on her lips. Her scent was intoxicating to him.

Meka became aroused, and her nipples fought to break through the soft fabric of her dress. She pulled her head back, and said, "Let's go, daddy. I'm starving." She massaged his dick over his pants, and wondered if he caught the double meaning of her words.

Twan nodded, adjusted his stiff dick, and smiled. On the way to the car, he smacked Meka on her soft, round ass, and noticed that she was panty-less. That only excited him more. He honestly wanted to skip the restaurant, and head straight to the house. But he wanted to make the night special for his lady.

Inside the car, Twan put on some old school Jodeci. *Every time I close my eyes, I wake up feeling so horny. I can't get you outta my mind, sexing you is all I need. I would do anything just to make you understand me - I don't give a damn about nothing else, freakin' you is all I need.*

"Oh, you thinkin 'bout freakin' me tonight?" asked Meka.

"Damn right," replied Twan.

"Well guess what, daddy. Tonight, your wish is my command." She gave him a smile that cemented her intentions.

$$$

At 9:33 P.M. Twan pulled up at the Red Dragon, an upscale Mandarin Chinese restaurant. They had the best oriental food in the upstate of South Carolina. Twan parked the car and put the top back up, and then he killed the ignition. When he opened the custom doors, they slid up, instead of out like every other car in the parking lot. An elderly white woman who was leaving the restaurant just stared with her mouth ajar, probably thinking she'd just been transported into the future.

Once inside the restaurant, Twan chose a table away from the crowd. He wanted them to have a little privacy. The tables in the restaurant were candlelit, adding a soft, warm effect to the establishment. Twan knew that would only enhance their dining experience.

Their waiter soon arrived at their table, and handed them both menus. They ordered appetizers to start out with, and glasses of white wine.

The couple made small talk, and exchanged sexually charged glances amidst the sensual oriental ambiance of the restaurant until their food arrived. When the waiter returned with their orders, he refilled their glasses with chardonnay.

Twan and Meka were eating, when over walked Rico, one of Twan's workers. Rico had his main girl with him. Her name was Tasha.

"What it is, Twan?" asked Rico.

"Ain't shit, Rico, just enjoyin' a lil' time out with my ol' lady, ya heard?"

"Hey Twan," said Tasha.

"What's up, Tasha, what's good?"

"I'm good. But you obviously ain't," replied Tasha, looking directly at Meka. "Not when you fuckin' with them 2-5 bitches."

Meka put her fork down, and said, "Hold up, you frog lookin', STD infested, broke ass slut. The next time you call me a bitch, you better be ready to fight, *bitch*! Don't hate on the District just because all you Fieldcrest bitches get A.I.D.S. while we get money!"

exclaimed Meka, loud enough for the whole restaurant to hear.

"Only reason half y'all bitches be gettin' any bread is 'cause you suck and fuck for it," retorted Tasha.

Meka lunged across the table at that bitch with a fork in her hand. Her plan was to stab her in the face with it, but Twan held her back. She knocked over their drinks in the process.

"Rico, get ya' girl, homey! I don't even appreciate her comin' over here wit' that bullshit, disrespectin' my lady while we out tryna have a good time."

"That's my bad, Twan. I just came over to discuss a lil' business wit' you real quick."

"Get at me Monday, my nigga. During business hours. This weekend right here is already reserved," stated Twan, glancing at Meka.

"Bet it up. Come on, Tasha," Rico said, snatching her by the arm.

"Nigga, don't be snatchin' on me! I ain't no muh'fuckin' doll!" Tasha looked like she was fuming on their way out of the restaurant.

A few minutes later, Twan noticed Meka wasn't eating. He asked, "What's wrong, Meka? Why you ain't eatin' the rest of your food?"

"That frog lookin' bitch done spoiled my appetite," said Meka, with a frown on her face. She just sat there playing with her food with her fork.

"Come on, baby, it ain't that serious."

On any other night, Twan would've been right. But it wasn't the comments that Tasha made that had Meka so upset. It was the fact that her and Rico would be able to say that she was the last person seen with Twan while he was still alive. But she told herself it wouldn't matter. Meka was ruthless when it came to men, so she dismissed those second thoughts fast. That nigga Twan was on the list, and it was going down.

She said, "Daddy, to be honest with you, I'm ready to go. Let's get outta here so I can go 'head and feed you yo' dessert." Meka licked her glossy lips, knowing that drove Twan out of his mind.

Just as she expected, he said, "Fuck it, lets ride." He dropped a crisp hundred dollar bill on the table to pay for the $72 meal, and cover a hearty tip.

They exited the restaurant, and headed to the car. After they got in, Twan peeled off toward his house.

Chapter 4

As soon as Meka and Twan walked through the door of his house, they were all over each other like two wild animals in the jungle. Twan de-activated the security system, and he was so pre-occupied with Meka he forgot to turn it back on after he shut the door. Meka peeped this, and smiled to herself.

Her performance as Twan's leading lady gave Oscar winning actresses a run for their money. But one thing she never had to fake with him was sex. When he ripped her little dress off and put his hand between her thighs, he discovered that she was already dripping wet. She was ready. His excitement showed through his pants. He fumbled with his belt, anxious to get inside of her.

Finally, with Meka's help, he got his pants undone and let them drop to the floor. Fully erect, he picked Meka's small but voluptuous frame up, and entered her roughly.

She clawed his shoulders, and screamed, "Oh my God!" His landing was rough, but she took it. Meka moaned and cried, "Fuck me, Twan. Fuck me, daddy. I wanna feel that dick, baby! Give it to me!"

She wrapped her thick brown legs around Twan's waist. Twan was pretty average sized, and he was trying to bang Meka's back out, but she acted like it wasn't enough. She screamed, "Harder! Harder, daddy! I wanna feel it!"

Twan obeyed, and thrust himself inside of Meka even harder.

Both of them were sweating profusely. It was too much. He yelled, "Oh shit, baby! I can't hold it, Meka, I'm 'bout to bust! Aahh, I swear! I'm 'bout to bust!"

Meka sucked on his earlobe, and said, "Bust that nut in me, daddy. I wanna feel it up in my guts."

As soon as she said that, Twan released his load inside of her. When she felt his penis softening, Meka caressed him and cooed, "Now let's go upstairs, so I can get you back hard, daddy."

After he caught his breath, Meka grabbed his hand and led him up the stairs to the master bedroom. As he ascended the lavish carpeted steps behind her, Twan could see his sticky semen sliding down her inner thighs.

Once inside the bedroom, Meka dropped to her knees and began giving Twan some brain. She used techniques she had seen in a few porno movies. She worked on his dick slowly, licking it and kissing it, all the while inhaling the musty scent of his sweaty balls. Seeing that it was taking him a minute to get back up, she decided to try a different strategy. She took Twan's meat out of her mouth, and positioned herself behind him, while still on her knees. She spit saliva into her right hand, and then Meka did something she had never done before. She placed her face between Twan's buttocks, and started licking his asshole, simultaneously using her hand full of spit to jack him off. She felt him jump with surprise, but she could tell he liked it.

Twan would have never let her put anything up his ass, but he had to admit he liked the rim job Meka was giving him. In fact, it was driving him crazy. In seconds, he was hard again, and ready to bust before he knew it.

Meka could tell he was close to the edge, so she worked her hand even faster. She still had her face buried between his ass cheeks, tornado tongue twirling his hole. The tickling sensation was driving him mad. That nigga had his toes curled.

"Goddamn, Meka, you killin' me, girl!" Twan yelled.

Meka stopped working his shaft, and gently squeezed his balls.

That pushed him over the edge. Spurts of semen skeeted wildly from his dick. Twan closed his eyes, and mumbled Meka's name over and over again, like he was in a trance. Damn, no woman had ever made him feel that way. He wanted to marry that girl.

Just then, two masked figures came through the bedroom door brandishing black pistols that matched their attire. Meka pretended to be too afraid to scream. Eyes wide with horror, she jumped up and grabbed a sheet, attempting to cover her naked body.

Twan was still in a daze, and physically weak from all the sex. He didn't even notice the intruders, until one of them smacked him on the back of the head with his pistol. "Yo Twan, what's up, my nigga?"

The force of the blow made Twan spin around. He was greeted by two faceless figures, both pointing pistols at his melon. Twan stared into the seemingly infinite holes of the barrels, and was paralyzed with fear. His bowels loosened, and his stomach emptied right there. Loose, hot shit traveled down his legs, and embarrassed him even more in front of Meka. The stench of his feces quickly permeated the bedroom. Twan's weakened legs gave out on him, and he fell back onto the bed. Everything happened so fast, he didn't know what to do, or say.

"Goddamn, nigga! You done shit on yo'self?!" asked one of the masked assailants rhetorically. "Look here, Twan, we gon' make this shit real simple, 'cause I swear to God I ain't tryna be smellin' yo' shitty ass all night! I'ma ask you some questions, and I want some honest answers, dig? All we want is the paper, nigga. We get that, and you live. We don't, and you die. See how simple that is." The man's voice was slightly muffled from the mask.

Twan was still in complete shock from the situation. He could only nod his head "yes."

"Alright, where's the stash at?" The masked man to his right asked.

Twan finally remembered how to move his lips and talk. He said, "Look man, I-I-I d-don't keep no money here at the house."

"Wrong answer," stated the masked man to his left. He already knew that was a lie. He walked over to the bed and began beating Twan mercilessly with the butt of his black .44 magnum. Twan balled up in the fetal position and tried to avoid any more damage to his face. It was already bleeding and swollen in several places. From the looks of it, his nose had to be broken because it was gushing blood.

"Now we gon try this one mo' time!" yelled the man who had just finished pistol whipping Twan. "Where the fuck the stash at!?"

"Man l-listen, I swear on my m-m-mama's life there ain't no money in here," Twan stuttered. His normally deep baritone had become a falsetto.

"Wrong answer," stated the other masked assailant. "It looks like he wanna be brave, and do this shit the hard way," the man said to his partner.

Meka finally spoke up. "Twan, please just give them the money! It's not worth our lives, baby!"

"You better listen to ya' girl, dog. She tryna save you a lot of pain and suffering."

Twan just remained silent.

"Look here, nigga. It's too late for you to be tryna play tough guy after you done already shit on yo'self."

Twan still refused to speak.

The masked man on the left said, "Alright, fuck it." He placed the pistol on the bottom of Twan's foot, and squeezed the trigger. Blood, bone, and pieces of flesh splattered everywhere, and Twan screamed at the top of his lungs. He sounded like a wounded animal being devoured by a hungry predator.

Now Twan realized the seriousness of the situation. It wasn't a game. Half of his foot was missing. He finally spoke, his voice quavering with fear. "It's… it's in the closet," he whimpered.

"Speak up, mothafucka! I can't hear you," the masked man commanded.

"It's in the closet," Twan said again, this time louder.

"Now we startin' to get somewhere," Ant D said, his words muffled by the ski mask he was wearing. Mike went to the walk-in closet and started searching for the safe. He turned on the light, and walked to the rear of the closet, and spotted the fireproof safe in the corner. He did an about-face, and said, "I found it."

"What's the combination," Ant D asked Twan.

Twan was weak from loss of blood, and totally demoralized. Now he only hoped to escape with his life, so he immediately gave his assailants the numbers: "45-62-89."

Mike went back into the closet and tried the combination Twan had just given them. The door to the safe popped open, revealing several large stacks of bills.

"Jackpot," Mike said, smiling to himself. He walked back out into the bedroom to retrieve a pillowcase to put the money in.

"What's up?" Ant D asked Mike.

"Everything good, my nigga. Let me put the money in this pillowcase so we can get the fuck up outta here," replied Mike.

"Meka, find something to put on, and go outside and get in the car," said Ant.

Twan thought he was hearing things. He said, "Wha... Hold the fuck up, how the fuck do this nigga know your name, Meka?!"

Ant D didn't give his sister a chance to respond. He answered for her. He pulled off his ski mask, and in the process, revealed his stone brown face, cold brown eyes, and murderous intentions. "I know her name 'cause I'm her brother, nigga."

"What the fuck?!!" Twan exclaimed. The surprise of what he'd just heard almost caused him to defecate on himself again. "Meka, how could you shit on me like this? I loved you," he said. Twan was so heartbroken, he still didn't fully realize that the moment Ant D pulled his mask off; he was already a dead man.

Meka was a cold bitch. She laughed in his face. "Nigga, you ain't love me. You loved this thang I got between my legs. At least you got a good nut before you died. So just be happy 'bout that."

When Mike walked out of the closet with the pillowcase stuffed with illicit funds, Ant D said, "Meka, go get yo' ass in the car."

Meka picked up Twan's tee shirt off the floor and put it on, and then she headed towards the bedroom door. She looked back at Twan and gave him a smile that was colder than a Polar Bear's toenails. "Bye, Twan."

Twan had a huge lump in his throat, but he managed to yell, "I'll see you in hell, you *triflin' ass bitch*!"

Meka laughed. "Well, since yo' ass goin' there first, make sho' you tell the devil I said what's up. You pussy ass nigga! And just so you know…the dick wasn't even all that," she said over her shoulder. She walked out of the bedroom, and down the stairs without another glance.

Ant D walked over to Twan, who was perspiring so much his whole body was soaking wet. He was trembling, and the stench of fear emanated from his pores. It mixed with the already overbearing stench of feces that permeated the room.

Sensing that his life was almost over, Twan attempted one last desperate lunge at Ant D, only to be met with a shot to the back of his head from Mike's black Glock 9mm. Fragments of his skull and brain matter flew all over the room, and Twan's naked body hit the carpet face up. Ant stood over Twan and fired two more shots from his .44 magnum into his face (or what was left of it). Ant knew Twan was already dead, but he felt the need to mutilate the nigga who'd been fucking his sister. That was some personal shit. He stared down at the bloody, mangled corpse, his ears still ringing from the deafening shots he had just fired.

Mike said, "Let's go, Ant D!" Ant snapped out of it, and they both hurried out of the bedroom, and down the stairs. Once at the bottom of the stairwell, Ant started pouring gasoline out of a gas can he had left downstairs upon first entering the house. "No evidence, no witnesses, no crime…" Ant D started.

"…No case," Mike finished. Ant D laughed, and struck a match and tossed it on the gas. The fire immediately began to engulf the house with an intense heat.

"Let's go, homey," Mike said. They both took off running, straight out the front door to the crack car that Meka already had started, and waiting to go. They jumped in, and they pulled out of the driveway slowly, leaving behind death and destruction in their wake.

Chapter 5

The ride back into the city from Twan's house in Easley was pretty silent. Everybody was lost in their own thoughts. Mike, who was behind the wheel of the old beat up Honda Civic now, was concentrating on making it back to Gloria's house in The District without getting pulled over by the police. They were fresh from an extremely violent crime scene, and riding in a vehicle with enough evidence in it to put all their asses in a concrete box for the rest of their lives. Or maybe even on Death Row, so the last thing anybody wanted to see was the blue lights of a police car.

He and Ant D's last encounter with Greenville County police was still fresh in Mike's mind, so he was being as cautious as possible. He obeyed every traffic law in the South Carolina driver's manual. Of course if they *were* stopped, whoever that unlucky officer happened to be wouldn't be eating donuts or drinking any more coffee. Not in that lifetime.

And though both Ant D and Mike had little fear of anyone wearing a badge, neither wanted the extra heat killing a pig would bring. Especially in the Deep South. So Mike stayed on point, and drove back into the city using mostly side streets and back roads.

Sitting in the backseat of the Honda Civic, Meka stared out the window into the night. Her eyes were looking at everything but seeing nothing. Her mind was reflecting back on the childhood that she and her brother never had. All because of their mother's extensive drug habit, and the many things she did to maintain it.

Meka and Ant D stayed on the move from one relative's house to another. They never felt at home, but found strength in the fact that they had each other. The instability and hardships that they faced at such young ages made them cold toward strangers, but drove them even closer together. To the point where they became inseparable.

Back in the day when the twins were twelve, they stayed at their Aunt Gladys' house for a few months in a neighborhood called City Heights. City Heights was an ironic name for a neighborhood whose people saw the depth of poverty and hopelessness daily. But that was the norm in most poverty stricken neighborhoods in America. And for some reason they all had names that implied serenity; like City View, Piedmont Manor, Jesse Jackson Townhomes, or The Gardens. Those names belied the harsh reality of those environments, which were really more akin to a jungle.

Meka, who wasn't even a teenager yet, had already begun to blossom physically, and attract lustful attention from men twice her age. One of those men was Gladys' boyfriend, Ray Ray. He would come home from work drunk, when he had a job, and comment on how sexy Meka was, while lewdly massaging his dick. But only when her aunt wasn't around.

It started with just small comments like that, but as the days passed, Ray Ray began to brush up against Meka's body in a sexual manner whenever they were close to each other. He would always say "excuse me" or "my bad" to make it seem as if it was an accident. But it began to happen so often that it became obvious that he was doing it on purpose. Pretty soon he became bold enough to start groping her breasts and behind whenever they were alone together.

In the mornings, when young Tameka and Anthony were at school, Ray would go into their room and rummage through Meka's dirty clothes for a pair of soiled, dirty panties that she had worn recently. Once he found them he would place them to his nose, inhale her scent, and jerk off until he ejaculated into the crotch of her underwear.

The days turned into weeks, the weeks into months, and Ray Ray became even more sexually aggressive towards Meka. And then one day, when nobody was home, he brutally raped her. He took her virginity and her innocence at the same time.

The first time he did it, Meka silently cried herself to sleep under the covers. She shared the same room with her brother but she didn't say a word about it. As time passed, the sexual abuse became so frequent Meka just internalized the pain. She had oftentimes wondered what she'd done to deserve the torment she was going through.

Meka's silence only emboldened Ray. One time while she was taking a shower, Ray busted in the bathroom, claiming he had to piss. He pulled his penis out, and then tried to pull the shower curtain back. Meka screamed, and Ant D came running in the bathroom.

He asked, "What's wrong, Meka? What's goin' on?" But by that time, Ray had already zipped up his pants, and was walking out of the bathroom like nothing had happened.

Gladys usually worked from 8:30 A.M. to 5 P.M. and barely paid the twins any attention. But she was still their aunt, so after months of silence, Meka decided to tell her what had been going on. Everything except for the fact that Ray had been repeatedly raping her whenever they were alone.

"Look, Tameka, I'm doing you and yo' brother a fuckin' favor by takin' y'all asses in, 'cause I know my sister is fucked up right now, smoking that shit. But you ain't fixin' to be coming in my house tellin' no fuckin' lies on my man, you hear!? Why would he want yo' lil' young ass anyway, when he's got this full grown woman right here," Gladys said, gesturing at her body. "Huh?"

"As a matter of fact — Raymond!" she yelled, calling him into the kitchen with her and Meka.

Ray walked into the kitchen and sensed the tension in the air. He knew there was going to be some shit because Gladys never called him by his full name unless she was pissed. But he also knew he could talk his way out of it. Gladys was weak. She wouldn't let him go nowhere. Not as long as he kept banging her back out every night.

Gladys said, "Ray, Meka here says that you been tryna push up on her. Is that true?"

"Come on, Gladys. Baby, I can't believe you even sittin' here entertainin' this bullshit. You know I love you, baby. What would I want with this young ass girl?! I can't even believe you accusing me of no bullshit like this," he yelled. Then he stomped out of the kitchen into the bedroom, and slammed the door shut behind him.

"See there, Meka! See what yo' lil' hot ass done started?" Gladys yelled at her niece. "Go sit yo' ass down somewhere, goddamn it! You little lying ass slut!"

Meka attempted to keep her emotions in check but she couldn't stop the tears from staining her pretty brown face. She just ran into the back room and closed the door behind her. She threw herself onto her bed, which was really nothing more than an old mattress on the floor with sheets on it. She cried into her pillow, hating the fact that her aunt would take the word of some no-good nigga she was fucking over that of her own flesh and blood.

While Meka lay on that mattress filled with pain and confusion, Ant D walked into the room and spotted his sister curled up in a ball crying her heart out. Her pain became his immediately. He lay down beside her and tried to comfort her, while at the same time trying to figure out exactly what the fuck was going on.

"Meka, what's wrong? Why you crying like this?" Ant asked his twin sister.

Meka remained silent, too ashamed to tell her brother what Ray had been doing to her.

Ant wouldn't give up. He said, "Meka, listen. You my sister, girl. We done been through too much together for you to start keeping shit from me now. What's going on?"

Finally, Meka broke down and told her brother about all of the sick shit Ray Ray had been doing to her since they had moved in with Gladys. Ant D's eyes burned with rage, and he wrapped his arms around his sister.

After months of being sexually abused by Ray, and being accused of lying by her own aunt, Meka was extremely vulnerable. She needed to feel the affection and unconditional love that her brother provided her. Her young heart yearned for it. She took one of his hands in hers, and slowly guided it between her thighs.

Once Ant realized what his sister was doing, he hesitated and started to pull his hand away. But the warmth emanating from between her legs began to arouse him, despite the fact that he knew it was wrong. Or was it?

Under the cover in darkness, the twins explored and shared each others' bodies for the first time. Afterwards, as his sister lay beside him snoring, Ant made a vow to himself that Ray would pay for what he had done to Meka. With his life.

The next morning, Meka told Gladys she was sick, and didn't feel well enough to go to school. Gladys called Lakeview middle school and explained the situation to the principal, Ms. Humbert. She said that her absence would be excused, provided that Meka did the make up work.

"Alright, Meka, go lay down and try to get some rest. There's some chicken noodle soup up there in the cabinet," Gladys said, on her way out the door.

Meka went back in the bedroom and lay down on her mattress. She was only wearing a small white tee-shirt and a pair of pink panties that showed off the thickness of her young, firm, still developing body. She left the room door open, knowing that Ray would see her lying there once he got up to use the bathroom.

In only a matter of minutes, Meka felt Ray's presence in the doorway. She peeked at him and saw him staring her up and down. She closed her eyes and brought her knees up to her chest, causing her pink underwear to wedge in the crack of her ass. The panties were so form fitting, Ray was able to see the outline of her young pussy lips through the thin cotton fabric. Her dark pubic hair was so bushy it was coming out the sides of the elastic.

Ray's blood began racing at the sight of Meka's young, fresh body lying there exposed to him like that. He began to drool, like the hound he was. The longer he stood there, the harder he got, until he felt as if he would explode with raging lust and desire.

Meka, eyes still closed, slowly placed her right hand down the front of her panties. She rubbed her fingers between her legs until they were moist, and then brought them up to her mouth and licked them. She didn't really know what she was doing, but she was pretty sure that Ray Ray's perverted ass was getting excited.

Ray could no longer control himself. Blinded by lust, he rushed into the room and fell on top of Meka, tearing at her panties with his right hand, and attempting to free his penis from the constraints of his boxers with his left. "You little slut! You freak! You nasty little bitch! I knew you wanted it! I knew you liked that shit!!"

Meka screamed, and Ant D emerged from behind the door with a butcher knife from the kitchen in his right hand. He plunged the blade into Ray's neck first. Blood erupted all over the room.

Meka tried to get out from under Ray but his body was too heavy. He had her pinned to the mattress. Ant D continued to stab Ray Ray over and over again, lost in a rage that would become as familiar to him as an old pair of comfortable slippers over the years.

Finally exhausted, Ant D stopped and pushed Ray's bloody, mangled corpse off of his sister. At the age of twelve, Anthony Davis had committed his first homicide…but it wouldn't be his last.

Meka got up from the mattress and embraced her brother. She was crying, and her tears mixed with the blood that was still fresh on both of their bodies…

Chapter 6

Feeling relieved that they made it back to The District without any complications, Mike parked the car three doors down from Gloria's house. He pulled in the driveway of an abandoned house that was run down and boarded up. He killed the ignition, and turned to speak to his best friend, who sat in the passenger seat beside him. "What you think we should do with the car?"

"Shiiit, we can leave this muh'fucka right here. We both got on gloves, so it ain't like we leavin' no fingerprints behind," Ant replied.

"Yeah, but if ol' boy report his shit missin', and the police get to lookin' for it, we don't want them muh'fuckas gettin' this close to the house."

"Now that I think about it, you right. That crack smoking nigga lil' Joe been known to do some bullshit like that too. Like a muh'fucka really wanna steal this old piece of shit," Ant D said, laughing.

He and Mike continued discussing the best way to dispose of the car without drawing any attention to the heinous crime they had just committed.

The sound of their voices drifted to the back of the car, interrupting Meka's sordid thoughts of her painful past. Tears had escaped her eyes without her even being aware of it.

Her brother and Mike's voices had interrupted her reverie. They rescued her from thinking about a childhood that had scarred her for life, and brought her back to the present. *At least it's still dark outside*, thought Meka, as she used the back of her hand to wipe away the salty trail of tears that had silently slid down her cheeks.

Realizing that she was only three doors down from her mama's house, she got out of the car and walked the short distance home. She was excited about her cut from the robbery, but she felt dirty, both physically and mentally. Meka wanted nothing more than to soak her tired body in a nice hot bath, and scrub away that dirty feeling.

"Hold the fuck up, Meka. Where is you goin'?" her brother asked.

"Where it look like I'm goin'? I need to wash my ass, and put some clean clothes on," Meka said, and continued to walk towards her mother's house. She was barefoot. The gravel and dirt against the soles of her feet reminded her of the fact that she had left a pair of $600 Jimmy Choos behind, rushing to get out of Twan's house. *Oh well. Looks like I'ma have to go shopping this week,* she thought to herself.

The thought of shopping always lifted Meka's spirits. Wondering exactly how much money was in that pillow case, she began to feel better already. She entered her mama's house, and cracked a smile, thinking of all the new clothes she would cop from her favorite stores at Haywood Mall that week.

"There she go again with that hot shit," Mike said to Ant D. "A muh'fucka can't tell her ass nothin'!"

"Yeah, I know, but shit, we good now, Mike. All the hard shit is behind us. And while we sittin' here bullshittin' 'bout what to do with this car, really all we gotta do is take this beat up piece of shit back to Lil' Joe in the morning. The main thing is gettin' rid of these clothes, and them hot ass pistols. 'Bout how many bodies you think on them shits now anyway?" Ant D asked Mike.

"Probably enough to get a nigga put on Death Row, or a few life sentences. They was already hot when I got 'em. And with all the niggas we done put under the dirt, it would be damn near impos-

sible to know fa sho'. But you right, these muh'fuckas got to go.
They too hot to keep holding… like we got licenses for these shits
or somethin'," joked Mike.

After rapping with each other for a few more minutes and ex-
ploring the possibilities, both Ant D and Mike decided that breaking the pistols down, scattering the pieces, and letting their clothes
go up in smoke would be the best move.

After mutually agreeing on what to do, Mike got out the car,
closed the door, and walked up the road to Gloria's house. Ant D
waited in the car for about ten minutes before grabbing the pillowcase out from under the front passenger seat. He buried his nose
deep inside the top of it and inhaled deeply, relishing the rich aroma
of the money. That was the smell of power. He became intoxicated
with the aroma.

Finally, he got out of the car with the pillowcase, and headed
toward his mama's house. He decided to go in through the back
door instead of the front like Meka and Mike had done, just incase
anybody was watching. Once inside, Ant D walked down the short
hallway to his room and dumped the contents of the pillow case
onto his bed.

Mike walked in behind him, holding a can of soda. He saw all of
those dead presidents staring back at him, and went fool. "We rich,
muh'fucka! We did it, nigga!" Mike yelled. "How much you think
all this shit is?" he asked excitedly.

His excitement was beginning to rub off on Ant. They had gone
from stealing food out of grocery stores, just to have the proper
nourishment to be able to think straight for the day, to sticking up
the local gambling houses, to putting the extortion down on weak
ass niggas. They had done credit card fraud, and kidnapped niggas for ransom. You name it. Ant and Mike's criminal history was
extensive. They only involved Meka when it was really necessary.

This lick was their biggest to date. They had set up and robbed
one of the city's biggest dope boys…and had gotten away with it.
Hot damn!

"I don't know how much this is, but we damn sho' fixin' to find out!" said Ant D, now eager to know exactly how much they had licked for too.

They both began to separate the money into stacks of 100's, 50's, and 20's, and count their individual stacks.

"Goddamn, nigga, go 'head and put some music on while we countin' this shit," said Mike.

Ant D got up and walked over to his dresser where he kept his Sony CD changer. After selecting disc #7, he turned the volume up on that classic Jeezy shit, "Thug Motivation 101."

The rough, gravelly sound of Jeezy's voice came blasting out of the surround sound speakers mounted strategically around Ant D's walls.

"*The world is yours, and everything in it/ it's out there, get on yo' grind and get it/ The world is yours and every bitch in it/ get out there, get on yo' grind and get it. Aaaaay*"

Ant D and Mike rapped along with "Mr. 17.5" while counting the blood money stacked on the bed.

Two and a half hours later, Mike counted the last stack of currency, and wrapped it with a rubber band, bringing the total count to 635,500 dollars. There wasn't any work inside the safe, but 635 stacks was more than they had anticipated getting from Twan anyway.

Tired and exhausted, Mike sat on the floor with his back against the bed. "Goddamn, that was a lot of work," Mike said.

"You ain't bullshittin'. It took mo' work to count that shit than it did to get it *from* that fuck nigga Twan," Ant D stated with a yawn. The exhaustion was evident in his voice, and on his tired face.

"Yeah, we been plottin' on that nigga for a lil' minute. I ain't think he would ever show Meka where the stash was at."

"Nigga, is you crazy? Man, there ain't too many muh'fuckas on the face of the earth that can resist my sister, dog. I knew as soon as she got down wit' that clown, that it was only a matter of time befo' she broke his lil' weak ass down."

Just then, Meka strutted into her brother's room. Fresh out of the tub, and smelling like Johnson and Johnson's baby lotion, she had on an old pair of orange Carolina High School gym shorts and a tank top, with her hair pulled back in a ponytail. Her eyes got big as quarters when she spotted the large stacks of bills on the bed. "How much was it?" she asked, anxious to get her cut.

"600 and some change," Mike said, his voice betraying the fatigue him and Ant D both felt. Neither one of them had slept much the past few days, staying up on No Doze, coffee, and pure adrenaline.

"So, how much is mine," Meka asked with her hand on her hip, alternating glances between Mike and her brother.

Ant D gathered up 150 of the thousand dollar stacks, and handed them to his sister. "That's 150 right there, sis. That's you. But Meka, don't be spending a whole bunch of paper right now. This shit is still fresh in the streets. Give shit a minute to cool down."

Meka completely ignored what Ant had just said. She started to argue for a bigger percentage, but ultimately decided against it. Besides, she knew if she really needed anything, her brother and Mike would hold her down. She went ahead and took the 150 grand, and walked into her room smiling. She was already making plans for the upcoming week.

It was now 3:30 A.M. that Sunday morning. The strain from the previous day's events was apparent on both Ant D and Mike's faces. They gathered the remaining money together, and put it in an old book bag of Ant's. Then they placed it in the back of his closet, under some old clothes.

"Tomorrow we gon' take lil' Joe's car back, and for the rest of the month, we just gon' lay and chill. See what the word is on the street, ya dig?" said Ant D, tiredly.

"I'm wit' that homey. Ain't no telling what type of fallout there gon' be behind this shit. But as soon as shit cool off, you know we gotta take these lames to class, and teach 'em how to stunt fa' real."

"Oh, you already know that, my nigga, that's mandatory. But

right 'bout now, I'm tired as fuck," said Ant, his words beginning
to slur. "We been up for damn near two days straight, so I'ma get at
you in the morning…or afternoon. Or whenever the fuck I get up.
Shiiiiiiiit, I might sleep all day tomorrow," Ant D yawned.

He lay down on his bed, not even bothering to get undressed. As
soon as his face hit the cool surface of the pillow, he was out cold.

Mike walked into the living room and stretched out on the thick
cushions of the black leather couch. He kicked his shoes off and
closed his eyes, playing back in his mind the numerous crimes that
he and his homey had committed over the years.

Like the time they had kicked in the door of a hustler by the
name of Dog barefaced, while his wife and young children were in
the house. Dog wasn't really a major player in the game, but it was
still a nice little lick for two young niggas trying to come up. They
had hogtied Dog and pistol whipped his wife until he broke down
and told them where the money and crack was at.

Mike's eyes closed as he took a sordid trip down Memory Lane.
Getting comfortable, he thought back on the first major lick he,
Ant D, and Meka had ever pulled together a couple years ago…

*"Everybody on the muh'fuckin' floor!!" yelled the two ski-masked
figures standing at the center of Greenville, South Carolina's First
Union Bank. Both men's attire was entirely blacked out. They wore
black hoodies, black cargo pants, and black Timberlands. Underneath
their hoodies, they wore lightweight Kevlar bulletproof vests that were
designed to protect law enforcement officers from high caliber handgun
rounds. Black leather gloves covered their hands, which were tightly
gripping AK-47 assault rifles. Their fingers rested on the triggers, ready
to squeeze at the slightest resistance to their demands.*

*"I said everybody on the muh'fuckin' floor! Y'all know what time it
is!"*

*A tall, heavyset, White man, conservatively dressed in a navy blue
business suit, looked at his watch as if that was a question. He was actually attempting to determine what the time was!*

"Man, get yo' stupid ass on the ground!" the robber yelled, while

pointing the chopper at him. Filled with fear, the White man's eyes got big, and his face turned beet red. He quickly dropped to the highly waxed bank floor, praying that he wouldn't be shot.

The taller of the two masked figures lifted the AK towards the ceiling and squeezed the trigger, letting off a barrage of high caliber rounds. The sound of gunfire filled the air, along with the heavy odor of cordite. Terrified screams of customers and employees filled the bank, and the few who were still standing dropped to the ground like sacks of potatoes.

It was 9:30 in the morning, so the bank had only been open for business for thirty minutes. There were very few people besides the tellers and managers inside, and that was exactly how the men robbing the bank wanted it. Fewer people meant fewer bodies they had to keep their eyes on.

On a job like this, there was absolutely no time to waste, so one of the masked men ran over to the long, marble teller's desk, and slid over the counter. His partner remained at the center of the floor, making sure nobody tried to be a hero. Behind the desk, lying face down on the floor were the three female tellers who regularly worked at First Union Monday through Friday. One was a heavyset, middle aged, Black woman. The other two were young White girls, fresh out of college.

Using his right hand to keep the assault rifle steady in his grasp, the ski-masked man reached down with his left, and grabbed a handful of soft blond hair. He jerked one of the tellers violently onto her feet. She screamed out in a combination of pain and fear. With tears beginning to ruin her make-up as they slid from her big blue eyes, she pleaded for her life. "P-p-please don't h-h-hurt me!" she sobbed.

"Bitch, shut the fuck up! Did I tell you to talk?"

What little color her pale face possessed immediately drained from it when she felt the barrel of his AK being jammed in her ribs. "Get a bag, and empty all the drawers into the bag. And hurry the fuck up!!"

Nervously, the young woman got out a thick, clear, plastic bag, and began to do as she'd been instructed. She hurriedly emptied the contents of the first drawer into the bag, large stacks of fresh hundreds, fifty's, and twenty's falling inside of it. She then moved on to the next drawer. She began to empty it, but her hands were sweating and shaking so badly that it dropped to the floor. Bills scattered everywhere.

She bent down to pick them up, but was interrupted by the masked figure holding her at gunpoint. "Next drawer! Next drawer!" Time was of the essence.

The other masked man who was standing guard in the middle of the floor glanced at his watch, and noticed that they were already fast approaching the agreed upon three minute exit time. "Two and a half, two and a half!" he yelled to his partner. They didn't have time to slow down.

See, what a lot of people fail to realize is that robbery is a science akin to boxing. If you didn't want to get your ass knocked the fuck out, or sent to prison for a long period of time, then you had to get in and out. Stick and move, stick and move. The longer you stayed in, the higher your risk of getting caught was.

With that thought weighing heavily on his mind, the masked figure behind the counter grew impatient. As soon as the young White woman was finished filling the bag with the fresh, crisp bills from the third drawer, he snatched it out of her hand, tearing off one of her French manicured nails in the process. He then half jumped, half slid back over the marble countertop. As soon as his hundred and sixty-five dollar boots hit the ground he was running for the exit; bag full of money in one hand, AK-47 in the other. His partner held down his rear until he was out of the bank, then he slowly backed his way towards the front entrance. Once he got to the glass doors, he turned and ran out of the bank too.

He sprinted to a dark blue, beat up Toyota Tercel that was already running. He snatched open the rear right door and jumped in. "GO! GO! GO!"

Immediately the car began to accelerate forward, and out of the parking lot. Not fast, not slow, but at a normal pace, so as not to attract the attention of any potential witnesses that would be willing to testify in court. The masked man on the passenger side reclined his seat all the way back, while his partner ducked down in the back to avoid being spotted from the windows.

The two masked robbers' hearts' were pumping fast, full of adrenaline. They both had to take a deep breath, and force themselves to calm down *after the rush they'd just gotten from robbing the bank. They had experienced a new high. One that could never be duplicated by any kind of drug.*

The robbers removed their masks and looked at each other, cracking Kool-Aid smiles. "Wooooo! We did it, muh'fucka!! We did it!!" The one in the back seat looked at the driver, and grinned at her.

The female driver glanced in the rearview mirror at him, and said "What the fuck is you cheesin' 'bout, nigga? What's so funny? You better be thinkin' 'bout my cut!" she said, her young voice belying her much older appearance.

"I'm just trippin' off that big crazy ass grey wig, and all that fuckin' make-up yo' ass got on," he chuckled. "Yo' ass look like a old ass woman fo' real," he said to the girl driving, who just happened to be his sister.

"And them goddamn glasses…" said the passenger. He couldn't even finish his statement before erupting into laughter.

The brown-skinned girl cracked a dimpled smile of her own as she took a glance into the rearview mirror at herself. The curly grey wig, heavy make-up, and large Coca-Cola bottle glasses she had on wasn't a disguise that would fool Stevie Wonder up close, but from a distance it made the woman appear to be much older than she was. The disguise had served its purpose. Laughing at herself now, she said, "Nigga, fuck y'all!"

Mike lay on the couch reminiscing on all of the crazy shit he, Meka and Ant had done over the years. They had been traveling on the long and hazardous road to riches for a minute now. With no regard whatsoever for the repercussions and possible consequences of their actions.

Over the years, Meka, Ant, and Ms.D had become the family Mike never had. The family he'd always wanted. And for his family, he would ride. And if it came down to it…die. As he drifted off to sleep, scenes from his extensive criminal career played through Mike's mind as vivid as a high definition Blu-Ray movie.

Chapter 7

Zulu calmly paced the floor of the empty warehouse, showing no signs of his emotions other than the murderous glare in his eyes. He walked with a noticeable limp, acquired from a shootout that had claimed the life of one of his closest comrades, Deemo, back in the day, and left Zulu in the hospital recuperating for months.

Back when he was young and trying to establish his reputation as a certified crazy mothafucka, which for him was far from an act, it was nothing for a gunfight to pop off. Or a knife fight. Or any kind of fight, for that matter.

Zulu was the color of burnt rubber, with a wide, flat nose that reflected the African tribe his parents had descended from. Wanting a better life for themselves and their unborn son, Zulu's parents migrated to New York in 1975. Like so many families, they were in search of that fabled American Dream. But instead, they only found American nightmares of discrimination and racial violence. That was the true reality of "America the Beautiful." Land of the free, home of the slaves.

The same year that they came to America, Zulu was born. His parent's tried to instill in him the traditional values and principles of their tribal roots, but the streets were calling. That was a call that turned out to be impossible for young Zulu to ignore. At the tender age of eleven, he answered. He became a lookout for the notorious Supreme Team, a widely known, infamous drug organization that ran Jamaica, Queens back in the day.

Over the years, Zulu gradually rose from a street corner lookout, to lieutenant in one of New York City's biggest drug empires. As time passed, his ruthlessness and cunning became legendary. To cross Zulu was not only a stupid move, but also a fatal one.

Once, an up and coming hustler from Harlem named Pretty Tony copped some weight from Zulu on consignment, and then brazenly refused to pay what he owed. It was obvious that either Pretty Tony was crazy as fuck, or he just didn't value his life that much. Either way, his ass wasn't pretty much longer.

Zulu was furious that a nobody ass nigga like Tony would even attempt to gain a rep off him. And since the beef was now personal, he wanted to be the one to exterminate that fucking roach himself. He would do it with his bare hands. Or maybe he'd torture Tony for hours, and then put him out of his misery. Zulu enjoyed torturing niggas. The sight of his enemies' blood draining from their worthless bodies excited him the same way some got excited watching their favorite football player score a touchdown. Pretty Tony would be no different.

On a cold Christmas morning back in '99, Tony's parent's received a very special gift on their Uptown doorstep, courtesy of Zulu. It was a large box wrapped in shiny gold paper, with a big red bow on top. Inside the box was what used to be Antonio Lamont Gray, his body chopped into numerous pieces of flesh and bones. Tony's mother fainted, and his father lost his breakfast.

The heat from the crime, which the authorities dubbed "The Christmas Massacre," caused Zulu to flee from N.Y. down south to Greenville, S.C. He chose Greenville because he had a few family members that were moving work he was sending down there.

After a few years of laying low, Zulu opened shop back up. Soon every narcotic coming through the southeast either came through his hands, or he saw a percentage of the profit.

So when his nephew and protégé' Twan was found brutally murdered and burnt to a fucking crisp, Zulu had no idea where the threat was actually coming from. Success bred enemies, so whoever was responsible was irrelevant.

Every nigga in the street knew that fear was the most valuable currency any man could have. Fear was more valuable than any amount of money. When people had no fear of you, then you became exposed to anybody with nuts big enough to try you.

And there were so many niggas at the bottom who were starving. They were just waiting for an opening. Any sign of weakness became an opportunity for them to eat. So Zulu took this affront to his organization seriously. Very seriously.

What troubled him more than anything was the fact that he'd introduced his sister's youngest son to that life personally. He'd watched Twan grow up from a snot nosed, shy little kid, into an intelligent, cunning young soldier. And now all that remained was his fucking ashes! Not even a fucking body to bury!

A trained warrior of the street, Zulu often saw ten steps ahead of his adversaries. He did this not by watching movies like "Scarface" and "Goodfellas" a hundred times, but by constantly educating himself on human nature, psychology, and behavior. He'd studied classics such as Sun Tzu's *"The Art of War"*, Robert Greene's *"The 48 Laws of Power"*, and Niccolo Machiavelli's *"The Prince."* Not to mention, Zulu was an avid chess player, and he tended to apply those same principles to his everyday life.

After hearing of Twan's murder, he immediately assessed the situation, and calmly determined that some lives would be lost behind it. Plain and simple. And their deaths would be particularly painful, to send a message to anyone else that might be lying in the cut scheming.

The rules of the jungle dictated that you were either a predator, or you got preyed upon. And Zulu had never been the type of man to be preyed upon. The streets were a game of chess, not checkers. Zulu played for keeps.

But now that he was older and less impetuous, Zulu felt little need to get his hands dirty in retaliation. Nor did he have to. He had a team of young guerillas who were always willing to prove their loyalty and mettle on the battlefield of the streets.

Amongst these soldiers, in an abandoned warehouse on the west side of G-ville, Zulu spoke. "I want to make this short, and to the point. I don't intend on repeating myself, so listen carefully," he said in his deep New York baritone. Just like his face, his voice reflected no emotion.

"As you already know, my nephew Twan is dead. What we don't know is who is responsible for his death. That means that at this very moment, our entire organization is vulnerable. This is not acceptable. I want the people responsible for this transgression punished…severely. But make sure it's the perpetrators who are dealt with. I do not believe in the innocent being hurt. It brings extra heat from the pigs, and it's bad for business. So if that occurs, then the individuals responsible will be dealt with accordingly. Understood?"

A group of about fifteen young men all replied in unison, "Yes sir!"

"Now…find out who was behind this, and deal with it. Oh yeah… there's a hundred thousand dollar reward for whoever adequately solves this problem to my satisfaction. Dismissed!"

Though Zulu had never explicitly mentioned anybody being killed, it was very well understood what type of results he wanted.

Chapter 8

It was Labor Day weekend, 2006. The last official holiday of what had been one of the hottest summers in recent history was getting ready to get even hotter. It was Saturday, September 1st, almost a full month since Ant D and Mike had capitalized off of Twan's weakness for Meka.

The police investigation was at a standstill, with little to no leads for the pigs to work. Officially the investigation was still open, but unofficially nobody in the Greenville County's Sheriff's Office really gave a fuck about another dead drug dealer. Especially a Black one. In fact, some of the officers were overheard making jokes about the condition in which Twan's body was found.

The word on the street was that some jack boys from out of state were responsible. All of this misinformation relieved Mike and Ant D's worries. They were getting restless with all that money just sitting around. They were ready to "ball 'til they fall." And what better time to ball than Labor Day weekend? Their original plan of opening a strip club was no longer even on their mind.

That night at about 10:45 Mike pulled up to Glo's house in his new '06 Cadillac Escalade. The truck ran him about 70 stacks alone, and not to mention the other 40 G's worth of customization he'd had done. The truck was all black, with chrome accents and chrome 28 inch TIS rims, wrapped in low profile Pirelli Tires. The steering wheel and dash were a rare rosewood color, and there were TV's in all the headrests and visors, and an Xbox 360 in the glove compartment. It had taken close to three weeks for all the work to be completed. And now that it was, Mike was ready to shine until mothafuckas went blind.

The baseline from the G-Unit song *Stunt 101* shook and vibrated the concrete, along with the windows of Glo's house. 50 Cent's voice blasted out of the speakers:

"I'll teach you how to stunt - My wrist stay rocked up, TV's pop up in the Maybach Beeeenz - I'll teach you how to stunt - Nigga you can't see me, my Bentley GT got smoke grey tiiiiiiiints..."

Ant D felt the bass all the way in the house, so he knew Mike was outside waiting on him. Glo walked into the living room just as Ant was getting ready to leave.

"What the hell is all that noise?" she questioned.

"Oh that's just Mike, mama."

"Well tell him to turn that shit down! What he tryna do, wake up the whole neighborhood?"

"We finna head out anyway, ma."

"Ok, well y'all boys be careful, alright?"

"Fa sho' mama." Fresh, dressed, and feeling like a million bucks, Ant D walked outside with his usual bop and hopped in the Escalade, taking in that new car smell. There were three types of scents that Ant loved: Money, new cars, and pussy. And usually in that order.

Mike turned to his dog, and flashed a smile that set him back another 40 stacks in diamonds and rubies. And it wasn't one of them bullshit ass grills that you could take out either. His shit was permanent. "Nigga, is you ready?" asked Mike.

"Muh'fucka, I came out my mama pussy ready!" retorted Ant D.

"Say no mo' then." Mike pulled away from the curb, and turned the volume up even louder.

At 11:46 they pulled into the parking lot of Platinum Plus, a strip club that contained some of the most exotic and beautiful dancers the upstate of South Carolina had to offer. Back in the day when it was simply a disco, it used to be called Characters. But mothafuckas acted up in there all the time and gave it a bad name. After so many incidents of violence, and even a few deaths, it was shut down.

The new owners had the building renovated, and turned into an erotic paradise that on any given night held at least 40 dimes. And on weekends and holidays that number jumped to anywhere from 50 to 70 women. Broads of all nationalities worked the large stage, the floor, and VIP room, getting their grind on, figuratively and literally. Being that it was a Saturday, the first of the month, and Labor Day weekend all rolled into one, the club was already packed beyond capacity. That meant that it would take a little extra cash to get them in.

Mike killed the ignition, but turned the key back in order to keep the music playing while he and Ant D pulled out plastic baggies full of some exotic shit they got from their weed man, Trap. They broke the fragrant buds down, and then rolled them in cherry flavored blunt wraps. "No seeds, no stems, no sticks, nigga," Mike said, and lit up.

"Yeah, this that good shit," Ant D coughed. "This that shit Bob Marley and 'dem dreads be burnin' down there!" Ant D took a deep pull, and held the smoke in his lungs as long as he could.

"Bob Marley dead, nigga," Mike quipped.

Ant D released the smoke, and said, "Yeah, yeah, you know what the fuck I mean though," he laughed, already feeling the effects of the potent reefer. "Dis 'ere smoke from 'de islands bwoy," Ant said, in his best (or worst) West Indian patois. Then he sang, *"Buffalo soldier... Dreadlock rasta..."*

Mike laughed, and said, "Nigga, you clownin'." He was also starting to feel the effects of the sticky green buds with fine white hairs on them.

After they had smoked for a while, and were feeling good, they decided that it was time to enter the club and see what was shaking

- literally. Ant D got out the truck first, brushing the remnants of ashes and loose weed off his new clothes. He checked his appearance in the side mirror, and rubbed the top of his head to make sure his waves were still spinning.

He nodded at himself in approval. Both of his earlobes held yellow diamonds in them the sizes of small pieces of candy. He had on a dark blue Polo shirt that made the diamond encrusted, gold Cuban link with iced out cross pendant he wore stand out even more. His jeans were a pair of $220 Evisu's, and his outfit was completed by the white and dark blue Nike's on his size ten feet. The large stacks of money stuffed in his pockets topped it off. After staying low profile for the past month, Ant planned on having fun that night.

Mike hopped out next. He was rocking a brightly colored Coogi shirt with a crazy ass pattern on it, the matching Coogi jeans, and a pair of custom dyed Nike Air Max. Around his neck was a platinum and diamond chain, with a diamond encrusted 9mm pendant dangling from it that he wore religiously. It wasn't hard to tell the Glock 9mm was his handgun of choice. There was a large rock on his pinky finger, and he wore a watch with so many diamonds in it you would've thought time froze. Mike was a little darker complexioned than Ant, so the bright colors he wore played nicely off his skin.

At 12:27, Mike and Ant D walked up to the door of Platinum and slipped security a few Franklin's. They did this for two reasons. First of all, and most importantly, to get them inside the packed club, which the Fire Marshall would probably have no problem shutting down. The second reason was that they wanted the guards to overlook their blatant disregard of the "business casual" dress code, and their ages as well. Neither of them was quite 21 yet, but money talked… Y'all know the rest.

Once inside, they bogarded a table close to the main stage, previously occupied by a couple of lames. One of the dudes looked like he wanted to protest, but the looks on Mike and Ant D's faces told the two older cats not to fuck with them crazy ass young boys. As soon as they were seated, they ordered four bottles of the establishment's best champagne in buckets of ice.

Once the champagne mixed with the weed…it was on. Mike started tossing hundreds of ones in the air at the girls on the stage, while Ant D took pictures with his camera phone.

It wasn't long before all the dancers noticed how big these two young niggas were doing it. The girls started getting open - literally. The stage held about five girls at a time, and two of them by the names of Strawberry and Diamond started putting on a freak show together directly in front of Ant and Mike.

Strawberry was a brown skinned Amazon with the measurements of 36DD-26-45. Her body was mean! And no ass implants either. Strawberry had Buffy the Body beat. And her face was prettier too.

Diamond was smaller, but still extremely thick for her short stature. She had 34c breasts, and nipples that stood erect like small pencil erasers. She had a caramel complexion, bedroom eyes, and thick, juicy lips.

Strawberry was laying on her back with her legs spread toward Ant D and Mike, who were transfixed by the scene playing out in front of their eyes. Diamond was on top of Strawberry in the 69 position, with her face buried between her thick thighs, licking and sucking her pussy through the thin fabric of her neon pink G-string. Strawberry opened her legs even wider in order to make sure the guys got a good view of her thick, meaty pussy.

The rest of the patrons at Platinum Plus were losing their minds at seeing those two beautiful women do their thing right in front of them like that. There were three other girls trying to work the stage, but Strawberry and Diamond had already stolen their shine. It was a wrap.

With her legs still wide open, Strawberry continued to get her pussy eaten until she finally came in Diamond's mouth. Diamond got up first, and licked her juicy lips like she enjoyed the taste of another woman in her mouth. She was immediately showered with numerous bills from all directions.

Strawberry got up next, and was also showered with an assortment of currency. She tossed her cum soaked G-string into Mike's
lap. The girls gathered their earnings, and headed off to the dressing
room to wash up and freshen up before they came back out and
worked the floor.

Just then, an old classic Mystikal club banger came blasting
out of the speakers. Five more girls got on the stage, shaking and
bouncing their voluptuous bodies to the rhythm. *"Girl, shake ya
ass!! Watch ya self!!"*

After the little show Strawberry and Diamond had just put on,
both Ant D and Mike were lost in a zone, ready to seriously fuck
something. Ant leaned across the table and yelled over the loud
music into his homey's ear. "Man, let's get some of these bitches
together, and get us a suite!"

"You know I'm' wit' it, my nigga!" Mike yelled back, his speech
slurred from the vast amount of alcohol he'd consumed.

Ant D felt a hand on his shoulder. When he leaned his head
back to see who it was, he found himself looking directly into the
blue contacts in Strawberry's eyes.

"Did you guys enjoy the show?" she asked, smiling seductively.

"I liked it so much I want an encore. In private," said Ant D,
pulling the thick stripper onto his lap.

"That can be arranged if you're serious," Strawberry drawled in
her deep Texan accent.

"Damn right, I'm serious, baby. As serious as a life sentence. But
I was wondering if you could get a few mo' girls together so we can
have us a lil' party somewhere."

"Like where? Where we headed?"

"Shiiiiiiiit, we gon let y'all pick the spot," Mike said, still slur-
ring.

"And what about the price? How much y'all willing to pay for
this lil' show?"

"Look," said Ant, "Money ain't no issue at the moment, so I

don't see no reason for you to make it one. Name the price, get ya' girls, and let's go. Fuck all this talkin'," he stated. He was ready to put all that conversation in a casket, and get inside one of those freak bitches.

Strawberry got up off Ant's lap, and left him with an erection that was harder than a brick. She licked her lips, and said, "It's gon' cost y'all $500 per girl. If you can handle that, then I know I can get at least 6 or 7 other girls to come with us."

Ant D reached into his pocket and pulled out several stacks of bills wrapped in rubber bands. He flashed them at Strawberry, and asked. "Why is we still talkin'?"

Seeing that those dudes were indeed serious, she told them, "I'll be back in a sec'." She sashayed back in the dressing room, making her ass shake and jiggle with every single step she took. She knew her every move was being watched by more than a few patrons at Platinum. Strawberry called that her Presidential Walk. It was the walk that got her the presidents that mattered most, the dead ones.

In the urban community, female adult entertainers, such as strippers, exotic models, and porn stars, were popularly looked upon as the female versions of hustlers. Just as their male counterparts were trapped by black market pharmaceuticals, the ladies mirrored their position, except their product was themselves. It wasn't about America's societal opinions, or its capitalistic hypocrisy. It was simply about dead presidents.

Chapter 9

Earlier that day, Meka was at Sylvia's, a hair and nail salon located off of Laurens Rd. Owned and operated by Sylvia Brown, Sylvia's was the spot where women from all over the upstate went to get the latest hairstyles. And the latest dish of 'hood gossip.

Sylvia was a big boned, light brown skinned sister who loved talking shit almost as much as she loved doing hair. Raised in one of the grimiest sections of Greenville called Woodland Homes, Sylvia saw her environment as an inspiration to succeed, despite what the crackers said about people from the projects being lazy and uneducated. She knew what the statistics were, but was determined to prove them wrong against all odds.

So after she graduated from Woodmont High School, she enrolled in Greenville Tech's cosmetology program. She went on to obtain her license in cosmetology, all while continuing to do hair out of her project apartment. So many women loved the way Sylvia hooked them up, that she soon she had more customers than she could handle by herself. She got the idea to open up her own shop, and hired some other girls who were nice at doing hair and nails too. Before long it was one of the top shops in the upstate with a steady clientele.

Being that it was Saturday, and also Labor Day weekend, all six of Sylvia's chairs were occupied. There were six other women waiting, and reading the latest assortment of magazines kept on hand at the shop, such as *Sister 2 Sister, Vibe, Black Hair, Essence,* and *XXL* to name a few. There was also a large flat screen television mounted on the wall, which was playing the latest Hip-Hop and R&B videos.

The shop was abuzz as usual, as the women talked and laughed about the latest events in the news. "Girl, did you hear how much money P.Diddy's baby mama Kim Porter is getting in child support?!" one of the women asked.

"Naw, how much?"

"$25,000 a month!!" the first girl exclaimed excitedly. "And that's just for one kid. There's twelve months in a year, so y'all can do the math on that one," she continued.

"Damn, she lucky. Why I can't never meet me a nigga who's rich like that?" wondered a woman who sat in a chair getting a pedicure.

"Forget 25,000…shiiiiit, I'd be happy just to get $250 from my triflin' ass baby daddy," stated another woman. The salon erupted into laughter.

"You ain't never lied, girl. Child, these niggas ain't got no problem coming around when they want some pussy. But as soon as you turn up pregnant, they act like they ain't have shit to do with *that* part."

"That's why y'all need to stop fuckin' with all them broke ass niggas! Y'all lowering the price of pussy out here for all the real bitches," joked Sylvia, who was finishing up Meka's hair.

"Shit, Sylvia, all the men that do get a lil' paper be goin' after them stankin' ass White girls anyway. It never fails. Once they money get right, they Black asses go White. They start chasin' behind them anorexic, pale ass bitches!"

"Sounds like somebody has some anger issues," joked another girl.

"I know one thing for sho', and two thangs for certain. If they keep fuckin' wit' them White girls then I'ma flip it, and find me a cute lil' White boy to take care of me."

"NO! Don't do that, sister. That's exactly what the White devil wants us to do! To lose hope in the Black Man, who is the foundation of the Black family, the foundation of the universe, and everything in it. He is the Sun, and we are the moons, meant to reflect their light and be their queens. Our whole race is being systematically targeted for extermination. We need to stand by our Black kings, and support their endeavors," said Niesha, whose boyfriend, Javon Taylor, A.K.A. Knowledge Born, became a member of the 5% nation of gods and earth's while he was locked up, and doing a five year bid in one of South Carolina's worst "corruptional" institutions, Lee County.

"There she go, there she go. Ever since Javon came home, you been talkin' that Black god, kill the devils, free the slaves, move back to Africa and live in a hut shit!" joked Sylvia. "That boy got yo' head fucked up, Niesha. Next thing you know yo' Black ass gonna be talkin' 'bout how a government conspiracy killed Pac and Biggie."

The whole room exploded in laughter again. "Using all them big ass words. I been to college, and still have to look up half the shit Niesha be saying."

Even Niesha had to laugh at that one. That was the thing about Sylvia. She talked shit but nobody really took her seriously. Even though most of what she said was true. She was like that older sister everybody had in their family that just said whatever came to her head. So instead of offending people with her comments, she usually just got them to laugh.

Meka was in her chair cracking up along with the other women. But after over two hours of sitting down getting her hair and nails done, she was anxious to get the hell out of there so she could set her Labor Day weekend off right. She had shopping to do. It was already one in the afternoon, and she still wanted to hit the mall and pick up a few items before that shit got packed. Young Jeezy was coming to town for a concert, and she planned to be the freshest bitch at the show.

When Sylvia said she was finished, and handed her a mirror, Meka quickly glanced at her reflection. Satisfied with Sylvia's work, she took out two hundred dollar bills to pay for her new hair style,

French manicure, and pedicure.

After paying Sylvia and saying goodbye to the rest of the women in the shop, Meka walked outside into the heat and bright sunlight of the early September afternoon. She stylishly put on her Gucci shades.

The sun kissed Meka's beautiful brown skin as she walked toward her brand new, custom painted, pink Range Rover Sport. She'd purchased it only days after Twan's murder, ignoring the advice of both her brother and Mike, who had told her to fall back and not spend any cash for a minute, until shit died down. But Meka said fuck that. She wanted it, and had the cash to get it, so she got it.

Humming the latest hit from her favorite singer, Keyshia Cole, Meka got to her truck, and reached in her Louis Vuitton handbag for her keys. Before she found her keys, a large arm wrapped around her neck from behind and lifted her completely off the ground. The culprit cut off her air supply immediately. Meka struggled against her assailant. Kicking and scratching wildly, she tried to break free of his hold.

Realizing her resistance had little effect, Meka remembered the .25 automatic that Ant D had given her a few months before. The gun was in her purse. On the verge of blacking out from lack of oxygen, she reached into her bag for the gun. Before she could retrieve it, she was savagely punched in the stomach by another man she hadn't even noticed. That blow knocked the remaining wind out of her, along with whatever fight she had left.

Her body went limp, and the two men quickly dragged her over to a black Dodge Caravan that was parked two spaces down. They got a roll of duct tape out of the van, and wrapped it around Meka's wrists and ankles. They put a smaller piece on her mouth, and then tossed her into the back of the van like a bag of trash. They jumped in, pulled the doors closed, and within seconds were speeding out of the parking lot.

Chapter 10

Mike pulled into the parking lot of the Hilton in downtown Greenville and brought the Escalade to a screeching stop. It was 2:03 A.M. The seven women in the truck who had left Platinum Plus with him and Ant D all breathed a sigh of relief at having made it to their destination in one piece. Mike was known for being a reckless driver. And that was when he was sober. So the weed combined with the alcohol only made shit worse. But now that they were there, it was time to get shit poppin'.

Ant D got out, walked into the brightly lit lobby and approached the clerk who was behind the desk. The middle aged, red necked woman didn't approve of his presence, but he was a potential customer so she hid her bigotry behind a smile that was as artificial as her nose and breasts. "Welcome to the Hilton, sir, how may I help you?"

"I want the best room y'all got."

"Well sir, we have a lot of beautiful rooms. Could you be a little more specific?"

"I want a room with a large bed, a livin' room, a sauna, and a nice view of the city."

"Alright, that would be a presidential suite. We charge five hundred dollars a night for that room, sir," the clerk said, the tone of her voice implying that she didn't believe he could afford such an expense. "Maybe you'd like something a little more in your price range."

"Naw, I'll take the suite," Ant D replied. He peeled five crisp hundreds from a stack and handed it to the woman, who hid her shock with yet another plastic smile. She took down information from his driver's license, and then gave him a room keycard.

"I hope you enjoy your stay at the Hilton, sir. If you need anything else, please feel free to call down to the front desk and ask for assistance."

As Ant D walked back across the lobby, she kept that fake ass smile plastered on her face and mumbled, "Damn drug dealers."

Back outside, Ant D told everybody that he'd gotten a Presidential Suite. The seven exotic dancers piled out of the Escalade, along with Mike, who was so drunk he almost fell on his face. The entourage walked through the lobby as Ant D led the way to the elevator.

Once inside the suite, Strawberry strutted over to the large stereo system, placed a CD in it, and pressed play. The sound of an old school R.Kelly song came out of the speakers:

"Sit down on the couch, take ya shoes off - Let me rub ya' body before I tear it off. Ya' homey lover friend is ready to flex - Girl fleeeeeex, time to have sex. Let's stop right here and work our way around - I won't stop until I hear that ooh aah sound. Don't front you know – about the rodeo show…"

All of the women began to get undressed and dance seductively, while Ant D and Mike sat on the plush leather sofa enjoying the view. They popped a few of the bottles of champagne they had ordered.

But before I go any further, I gotta describe the other five dancers who had come along with Diamond and Strawberry. These weren't just everyday chicken head, bird ass bitches that you found in them hole in the wall strip clubs. All of these bitches were official.

First there was Angel, a short, thick, Puerto Rican mami with naturally curly hair, and a face that niggas would die - or kill for. Angel was twenty-two, and a certified freak with a butterfly wing tattooed on each ass cheek. Whenever she was in the club and made it clap, it appeared as if the butterfly was actually flying! That skill often got her showered with currency. Niggas loved that shit! Angel had a group of regular patrons who were seriously obsessed with her. They'd fuck a nigga up over her. What made it so crazy was the fact that not one of them was even fucking her!

Next up was Chocolate, who got her stage name from the smooth dark complexion of her skin. Chocolate had large titties, and an ass like Serena Williams that jiggled and bounced whenever she did her little fuck walk. She had starred in a few porn videos, and had even been passed around like a blunt on the set of a few rappers' videos.

Then there was Obsession and Chanel, who were best friends but lied and told everybody that they were sisters. Obsession and Chanel were both light skinned, and had long, naturally wavy hair. Neither one had an ass worth going crazy about, but they had nice little bubbles for their frames. They both also had rings in their tongues, navels, and clits. And for the right price, they had no problem letting you see all three of them.

Last but not least, there was Anna, one of the few white girls working at Platinum Plus. Anna was raised down in Miami, in one of the worst sections of Dade County. So she was at ease with being around Black people. In fact, both of her baby's father's were Black. White men who came to the club often asked her, in private of course, what she saw in the Black men that she dated. Anna would simply reply that Black men's dicks were bigger, then sit back and laugh to herself as the White men turned crimson with embarrassment.

Mike, who by now was fully aroused, got up from the couch and grabbed Chocolate, Angel, and Diamond by their hands. He led the three of them to the master bedroom. Ant D stayed in the large plush living room with Obsession, Chanel, Strawberry, and Anna.

Once in the bedroom, Mike took his clothes off and lay down on the bed. The girls, who were now completely naked also, followed his lead. They got on the bed with him, ready to please. Chocolate grabbed Mike's stiff dick and kissed it affectionately, making loud smacking sounds. Angel joined in, and soon they were both slobbering all over his dick and balls, soaking his hard on with their wet, sticky saliva. Whenever he was in one's mouth, the other would alternate and take his balls in her mouth and start humming on them. That trick sent vibrations of pleasure throughout his body.

Diamond felt left out of the action so she started playing with Angel's pussy while she and Chocolate took turns pleasuring Mike. They were giving him the best head he'd ever experienced in his young life.

Their head game was so intense that, in only a matter of minutes, Mike exploded. Angel, who happened to be the one with his meat in her mouth at the time, got a mouth full of semen. Angel was no rookie at giving head, but she was a little surprised by how much cum he had skeeted in her mouth. His hot, sticky seed spilled out of her mouth, and ran down her lips and chin.

Mike opened his eyes and looked at Angel's pretty face soiled with his cum, and decided to take a flick in order to capture such a beautiful moment. He rolled over and grabbed his phone from out of his pants, which were on the floor beside the bed. Seeing that Mike wanted pictures, Angel, who always ready to perform, began to gargle and blow bubbles with the cum in her mouth. Chocolate and Diamond got in on the act, and started kissing Angel in the mouth. They all shared Mike's cum, while he continued snapping away with his phone.

Meanwhile, back in the living room area it was going down. Ant D had Strawberry bent over the couch doggy style, banging her back out. "Yeah, take this dick, girl. Take this dick," Ant D said each time he stroked inside her wet, juicy pussy.

She was throwing her big ass back at Ant D, giving him all he could handle. Anna was underneath them alternating between licking Strawberry's clit, and sucking on Ant D's big sweaty nuts. The smell of their sex filled her nostrils, and drove her wild with lust.

"Oh shit, I'm 'bout to bust," Ant D stated midstroke. Right before he climaxed, he pulled his dick out of Strawberry's sopping wet pussy, pulled the condom off, and skeeted between her ass cheeks. He fell back on the couch, exhausted and out of breath.

Obsession and Chanel, who had witnessed the whole scene from the other couch, were now both completely wet and ready for some dick themselves. Chanel got up and switched her ass over to Ant D. As her naked body got closer, Ant noticed she had something in her hand. Once she was standing in front of him he saw that it was a bag of white powder and a miniature gold spoon. She dipped the spoon into the bag and scooped up a little bit of powder, and offered it to Ant.

He made a face, and said, "What the fuck that is?"

"A lil' somethin' that'll get that big dick of yours back hard real quick, so you can fuck the shit outta me. And it'll make you cum harder than you ever came in yo' fuckin' life! I promise."

"Yeah, but yo' ass still ain't told me what the fuck it is," said Ant.

"Just a lil' coke, baby." She leaned forward between Ant's legs and placed the spoon directly under his nose.

Ant thought about what she said. He wanted to fuck all of those bitches and get his money's worth. And he didn't want to seem like he was a sucker, so Ant took the white girl up one nostril first, and then the other. Almost immediately, he felt the most intense, most beautiful feeling he'd ever experienced in his life. It was love at first snort.

Pleased that the narcotic had given Ant such an intense high, Chanel put a little bit of cocaine on the tip of his semi-limp dick. She hungrily took him in her wet mouth and sucked him back to attention, using her tongue ring to stimulate the tip of his dick. Though he had just squeezed one off, it only took Ant D a minute to get back hard with the expert techniques that Chanel was using.

By now, Strawberry and Anna had rolled off the couch and onto the floor, completely lost in their own world of lust for one another. Obsession saw that her friend had gotten Ant D back hard, so she gently pushed him back on the couch. Chanel mounted him, and slid his rock hard dick inside of her already well lubricated hole. She began to ride him reverse cowgirl, with her back to him. She started off real slow, and then started going faster and faster, until her body was just a blur of movement.

Since the dick was already occupied, Obsession decided that she would sit on Ant's face and let him eat her. Chanel turned around on Ant D's dick midstroke to watch her best friend get her hole eaten out. That turned her on even more. She never missed a stroke. So while Ant's face was buried between Obsession's meaty pussy lips, Chanel continued to ride him, up and down, down and up, while she observed the action. She pinched and rubbed on her nipples, enjoying the way his cock stretched and filled up her insides. Suddenly Chanel arched her back and let out a piercing scream, lost in the ecstasy of an orgasm so intense she sort of blacked out for a few seconds.

Once Chanel came back to reality, Obsession motioned for her to switch positions with her. They switched places, so now Chanel's cum soaked, sweaty pussy was riding Ant's face, while Obsession rode his dick side saddle, and gently squeezed his balls.

The three of them went on like this for a minute, until Obsession felt Ant D's body tense up. She knew he was almost ready to cum again, but she didn't want him to. At least not in her pussy. She hopped off of his erection right before he was about to let go, and laid down on the carpeted floor doggy style.

Her pussy was on fire, but Obsession was the type of freak that got off with a hard dick in her ass. She put her face down on the carpeted floor and stuck her ass up in the sex filled air, exposing her tight little asshole. "I want that dick in my ass," she told Ant. "Put it in my ass, baby."

Not believing his ears, Ant D was quick to oblige. He was so far gone that he had thrown all caution to the wind. He didn't even bother to strap up. That was a roll of the dice when fucking with any girl, but especially that type of bitch. A nigga never knew if he'd crap out and catch something. But caught up in the moment, Ant didn't even give a fuck. That coke had him feeling like a fucking porn star, like he could go on forever.

He'd had many sexual exploits with numerous girls, but had never fucked one in the ass. He got down on the floor behind her, and spit into her ass crack to add lubrication before he entered her tight hole. Obsession reached her hands around and spread her ass cheeks open, and Ant slowly entered her. As her asshole relaxed and began to stretch, he sped up the pace of his thrusts like he was trying to drive her face through the floor. Obsession loved his aggression. She started moaning, and then it sounded like she was speaking in tongues and shit.

After a few minutes of raw anal sex, Ant D was ready to release his load. Obsession knew it so she squeezed the muscles in her asshole to push him over the edge. He started shaking, and closed his eyes and ejaculated violently inside of her ass. Chanel was right, that was the most intense orgasm he had ever experienced in his entire life. He grabbed Obsession's waist, leaned forward and put his tongue in her ear.

With his seed filling up her insides, Obsession started climaxing herself. Her body bucked like a wild bronco. She closed her eyes too, relishing in the pleasure of her orgasm.

Chapter 11

Mike woke up the next morning with a foot with red nail polished toenails in his face. He had a splitting headache, and a dick that felt sore as hell. For a moment, he couldn't remember exactly where he was, or how he had gotten there for that matter. But the previous night's events came back to him slowly. Despite the headache, he cracked a smile at the thought of his first foursome. He had read in some magazine a while back that group sex was overrated. But either the dude that had written the article was gay, or he had fucked some ugly ass bitches, because the episode that had went down the night before was off the mothafuckin' chain!

Mike rolled over to his left and looked in Angel's face. It was early in the morning and she was wearing no makeup whatsoever, but her little Puerto Rican ass was still sexy as fuck. *I see why niggas be stalking her* thought Mike. *If she wasn't such a dog for any nigga with cash, she'd be wifey material,* he continued thinking, as she snored lightly beside him.

Mike sat up, and reached over Angel's honey brown body to retrieve his boxers off the floor. He put them on, got out of the bed, and headed to the bathroom. Once inside the bathroom, he took an early morning piss, and then got some Tylenol out of the medicine cabinet. He was glad to see those painkillers. He popped about eight into his mouth, and then washed them down with a shot of liquor from an almost empty Hennessey bottle that was sit-

79

ting on the sink. He didn't remember how it had gotten there, but was thankful that it was.

He walked into the living room area to check on his homey Ant, who was still knocked out. "Goddamn, it look like a bomb done went off in this muh'fucka," Mike said to himself, chuckling. Ant D, Chanel, and Obsession were all on the couch unconscious and completely naked, their bodies intertwined with one another. Strawberry and Anna were both passed out on the floor. Mike looked around and noticed near-empty champagne bottle after bottle, plates of half eaten food, and women's clothes and underwear scattered everywhere. The coffee table had a couple of straws and lines of white powder on it, which he figured was coke. He knew that neither he nor Ant had brought any with them, so he figured one of the girls brought her own little party stash from the club the night before.

Mike walked back into the bedroom to get his phone so he could take some shots of the disaster area back in the living room. As he walked back into the room, he saw Diamond's naked body leaning over the bed. Her hands were going through the pockets of his Coogi jeans. Mike couldn't believe that bitch. He said, "What the fuck is you doin'?"

She jumped, and dropped the pants. "Oh, hey Mike, I was just tryna find your phone so I could see what time it is."

There was a digital clock on the night stand right beside the bed, and eight or nine G's still left in his pockets, so it wasn't hard for Mike to peep game. "See, that's what I hate 'bout you triflin' ass bitches. A muh'fucka pay y'all, and you still be tryin' some slick shit on a nigga."

"First of all, I ain't no *bitch*. Nigga, you must got me confused wit yo' stank ass mama!"

Before Diamond could realize the mistake she'd just made, Mike was across the room with his left hand wrapped around her neck, and smacking her repeatedly the right one. It wasn't the attempted larceny that had set Mike off, but rather the comment Diamond's slick ass had made out the side of her neck about his mama. Ever since he had learned the truth about his mother, which was that she had died while giving birth to him, he made it his business to make anybody who said anything wrong about her regret it. And just because Diamond was a girl didn't mean that she got a pass. Fuck that.

Mike continued slapping her in the face, which caused her lip to split open, and her nose to start bleeding. Diamond tried to scream, but had no air in her lungs to do it with. Mike was strangling her to death!

All the commotion woke Angel and Chocolate up. Angel rolled out of bed and jumped on Mike's back to try to keep him from doing any more damage to Diamond, but this only caused him to turn his rage on her. Chocolate screamed. In a second, everybody was up in the suite trying to keep Mike from killing Diamond and Angel.

Strawberry, who was probably the heaviest out of all the women, jumped on Mike's back next. She held his arms in order to restrain him, and stop him from swinging.

Ant D finally came running into the room to see exactly what the hell was going on. He would've been in there sooner but he was so disoriented when he first awoke, he couldn't find his clothes. They were scattered amongst all of the discarded items on the floor. And plus, he took a second to take a quick snort from the coke that was lying on the table.

Once he entered the room and peeped what the fuck was going down, he yelled out to his best friend, "A Mike, chill yo' ass out, nigga! Calm the fuck down!"

Suddenly there was loud banging on the door, accompanied by the male voice of hotel security. He said, "I just want y'all to know that the police have been called. We don't tolerate this kind of behavior at the Hilton!"

Everybody in the room froze like they'd been put on pause, and then they started scrambling all over that hotel suite like Mike Vick with two defensive ends on his ass trying to get a sack. There was too much illicit shit in the room to be sitting around waiting for the police to show up. Nobody felt like sitting in one of them nasty ass holding cells, courtesy of the Greenville County Detention Center, for the rest of Labor Day weekend, until a judge showed up on Monday morning for a bond hearing. Everybody grabbed their shit and ran out the room to the elevator. Some of the girls were still half naked, struggling to get their clothes on.

Chapter 12

That same Sunday morning, while Ant D and Mike were scrambling out of the hotel, Meka was finally coming to. She had been unconscious for nearly a whole day, and her kidnappers were beginning to get worried that maybe she had slipped into a coma, and wasn't going to wake up. They all knew Zulu wouldn't tolerate any innocent people being hurt.

Until they found out a little more information, Meka was still potentially innocent. The only way to get that info was to apply a little pressure, and question her to find out exactly what she knew about Twan's murder. They couldn't question a corpse, so they were all relieved when Meka finally opened her eyes.

Rico was almost positive that he'd made the right move by kidnapping Meka and bringing her there. In his heart, he had no doubts that she'd had something to do with Twan's murder. All he had to do was prove it. He vividly recalled the last conversation he'd had with Twan at the Red Dragon. Twan had implied that that weekend was reserved for Meka. It wasn't any coincidence that Twan turned up dead that same night. Niggas in the streets didn't believe in coincidences. Not the smart ones anyway.

Rico was both young and full of cum, but he was far from dumb. So when he got word about the large purchases, particularly that custom pink Range, Meka had been making right after his homey's death, he put two and two together. He could've went to Zulu right then with what he knew, but he wanted to make sure he was absolutely positive before he made a move.

He knew from what he'd heard in the streets that Meka wouldn't hesitate to set a nigga up. But she had to have had help to get at Twan, and Rico wanted to know exactly who was involved with the hit. So he got together with a couple of other niggas on Zulu's squad, by the names of Ty and Black. He told them both what the business was, and what he wanted to do in order to find out exactly what the fuck went down that night. He told them he would split the reward money Zulu was offering with them.

Black and Ty were basically hand to hand, low level workers in Zulu's organization, so they were both ready to ride with almost any idea that would bring them more notoriety, and help them rise in the chain of command. Besides the reward Zulu had put out there, it was pretty common knowledge that he valued those with the ability to take the initiative to come up with the results he wanted.

Ty and Black had an abandoned house on Perry Ave. in West G-Ville. It was used to serve the fiends, and occasionally trick a few of the pretty young bitches that had fallen victim to whatever itch they had that needed to be scratched. Whether it was that girl, that boy, pills, dust, or even exotic weed. Whatever it was, Ty and Black made sure those young and naïve young girls got it. For the right price, of course.

The same bed that they used to trick on was what Meka was currently strapped to, spread eagled. Her wrists and ankles were tightly tied to each bed post with rope. Rico had stripped off all of her clothes, except her see through lace panties and matching bra, so she might as well have been naked.

As soon as she regained consciousness, Meka began to struggle wildly to break free from her restraints. But seeing that this only wasted energy and tightened the ropes around her wrists and ankles, she stopped.

Breathing heavily, her chest heaving, Meka looked around the room before she addressed the three men surrounding the bed. She noticed they were each wearing black bandanas to disguise their identities, and said, "Look, I don't know who the fuck you niggas is, or what y'all want, but it's obvious y'all got me fucked up wit' somebody else. So if you'll just go 'head and let me go…"

Rico cut her off midsentence. "Naw, we ain't got you fucked up wit' nobody, bitch! And hell fuck naw, we ain't finna let yo' ass go! At least not until you answer a few questions."

Meka wasn't sure but she thought that the man's voice sounded familiar. But it was kind of hard to tell with him wearing that black flag. At the top of her lungs, she yelled, "Look, mothafucka, I ain't answering shit! Fuck y'all niggas!"

Rico had figured it wouldn't be easy to get the information he wanted from Meka, so he wasn't really surprised by her little outburst. But right then was the perfect opportunity for him to establish who the fuck was in charge of that little show.

He walked over to Meka. Even in her current condition, he still couldn't help but admire her beautiful body. But when he thought of how she had used that same body to probably set Twan up, his anger overrode his lust. Twan was one of the few older niggas in the game he respected. He pulled his fist back and savagely punched Meka in her pretty mouth, splitting both of her lips. The coppery taste of blood filled Meka's mouth but she refused to swallow it. Instead, when Rico leaned in close to ask if maybe she had reconsidered answering his questions, she spit the blood out in his face and smiled.

For a moment, Rico was shocked at the audacity of that crazy ass bitch. Here she was, kidnapped, strapped to a bed with only her panties and bra on, and she still had the heart - the *gall*, to spit in his face?!!

Rico quickly regained his composure, and he started pounding on Meka's face and body nonstop, while Ty and Black looked on. Minutes later, Rico stopped beating on her only out of sheer exhaustion. Both of her eyes were swollen shut, and her nose and jaw were broken from the force of Rico's blows. Her lips were severely disfigured, and her top four teeth had been knocked down her throat. They were now being digested in the bowels of her stomach. Her once beautiful honey brown face was now just a mess of bloody flesh, bruises, and broken bones.

This definitely wasn't part of Rico's plan, but when Meka had spit blood in his face his emotions got the best of him. That "plan" shit went out the window real quick. Now that he had calmed down, Rico could see that he'd overreacted. Now it would be impossible to get anything out of Meka in her current condition.

Ty and Black looked at Meka's mangled, bloodied face, and then looked at Rico like he had just lost his fucking mind. Not because they gave a fuck about Meka, but because they were concerned about their own lives. They had no idea how Zulu would react once he heard about that shit. They weren't even sure she'd had anything to do with Twan's death.

Ty spoke first. "Rico, what the fuck is you doin', nigga? What's wrong with yo' ass? You said we wasn't gon' hurt this bitch, but just ask her a few questions, and shit. Now look at her ass layin' up in here with one foot in the grave. This here wasn't part of the script, nigga."

"Yeah, well sometimes you gotta adlib, muh'fucka! You seen that bitch spit in my face, dog! You seen her! I just lost it," Rico explained.

"Man, you know Zulu said he wanted for us to find out who killed his nephew, and handle it. He said he ain't want no innocent bodies poppin' up behind that shit," Black chimed in. "If she ain't had nothin' to do wit' Twan gettin' killed, and he find out 'bout this shit, we gonna look worse than her ass!"

"Look, I know what the fuck Zulu said, nigga! Everybody just calm the fuck down," Rico said. "Shit ain't that complicated. All we gotta do is get rid of this bitch body, and we good. And if y'all can hold water, then we ain't got shit to worry bout, ya dig?"

"That shit sound real good, but how do we get rid of a body just like that?" asked Ty.

"I already got that figured out. But before we do all that, we might as well have a little fun," said Rico, with a smirk on his face. He ripped off Meka's panties and bra.

Despite the fact that her face was swollen, bruised, and unrecognizable, as soon as her flesh was exposed to the three men in the room, they all became excited. They started feeling on her breasts, between her legs, and all over the rest of her naked body. They figured that she was out of it. Even in her current state, niggas wanted to fuck Meka.

They had no idea that Meka was still very much conscious, and had heard their every word, including their plans to dispose of her body. She lay there on that bed as still as possible, hoping that Rico and them other two clowns with him wouldn't go through with what they were planning. But it was only wishful thinking because she felt her ankles being cut free. She knew what time it was. They were going to rape her before they killed her.

It was pointless to struggle against them, so Meka just lay there as they each mounted her body and savagely violated her in every way, in every hole possible. She allowed her mind to travel to that same secret place it used to go when Ray Ray used to sexually molest her. Her body was there, but her mind was in a place far away.

"That's what I'm talkin' 'bout! Beat that pussy up, Ty!"

They no longer felt the need to conceal their faces with the black flags. They planned on killing Meka anyway, so they removed their bandanas and continued to ravage her body, while enthusiastically cheering one another on. Every time one was finished, another would hop on top of her and violate her with even more violent thrusts.

After what seemed like an eternity, but in all actuality was only around thirty minutes, Rico, Ty, and Black were through. Meka's thighs and pussy were sore, and soaking wet with a mixture of semen and blood that had pooled beneath her. To further add to her humiliation, they each jumped up on top of the bed and took turns pissing on her face. The warm, rank fluid soiled Meka's once beautiful face, and mixed with the tears that slid silently from the corners of her swollen eyes. And then she lost consciousness again.

Chapter 13

Every 'hood in every city across America had a place where everybody went on the weekend to get their shine on. A spot where the ghetto celebrities came out just to let muh'fuckas know they were still in the game – *BALLIN'!*

Greenville, S.C. was no different. On Sunday afternoons, everybody who was anybody in the Ville's underworld could be found at Cleveland Park. They got their stunt on in the latest vehicles, jewelry, and fashion of the season; the majority of which was purchased with blood money soiled with the stench of drugs. And it went without saying that whenever the ballers came out, the groupies, cheerleaders, and dick riders weren't far behind.

It was the final day of Labor Day weekend, and since the weather was good, and the sun was shining, the park was jumping a little more than usual. Young hustlers and gangstas from every 'hood were on hand to represent. Shit was crazy!

You had Lil' Money out of District 25 (which was a 'hood comprised of numerous different 'hoods like Piedmont Manor, The Valley, Bell Meade, Augusta Hills and Crosby Circle to name a few). Lil' Money was the son of one of Greenville's most notorious hustlers named Big Money, who was currently serving a life sentence in a Federal penitentiary in Ohio for killing an undercover federali back in 1990. Lil' Money never really got the chance to know his pops but he'd heard enough stories about him to feel like he did.

And you know what they say about the apple not falling too far from the tree.

Then you had an official certified crazy muh'fucka named Nut. The name was short for "Nut Nut." That's what the kids used to call Travell Noriss back when he was in elementary school. Like so many young Black kids with behavior problems, the teachers relegated him to the mentally challenged classes because they didn't want to be bothered with him. So the kids used to tease him and call him a "nut nut." That is, until he got tired of that shit, and stabbed one of them in the eye with a pencil. Ever since then, niggas just started calling him Nut because of his violent behavior.

Nut was from West Greenville, another grimy ass section of the Ville. He had just recently gotten out of Greenville Memorial Hospital, after being shot four times in front of Escalade, which was a new night club that had just recently opened. Nobody had really seen the niggas who had shot Nut, and with as many enemies as he had accumulated over his many years of being a bully, it wasn't likely that he'd find out who the assailant was any time soon.

There were two sisters from Brutontown, Shell and Neesy, who pumped that exotic harder than anybody in Greenville County. Purple, Dro, Kind Bud, Chocolate…whatever kind of trees you wanted, they had it on deck. Shell's boyfriend, Hector, was a member of the notorious Mexican Mafia, so it was nothing for Shell and Neesy to keep pounds of that good shit bagged up. Being that their supply was so easily accessible, they could afford to drop their prices lower than the competition, and still make money.

Red from Freetown was also up in the spot. Red was an up and coming hustler/rapper in Zulu's organization. His mind was sharper than a razor, and his heart colder than ice in the Artic. Word on the street was that he was next in line to take over Twan's former position on the team. Red was a workout fanatic. Since he stayed in shape, he tended to keep his shirt off. He liked to show off his muscles, and the tattoos he had gotten while bidding in some of the most violent penitentiaries in S.C. like Lee County, Libre, and

Evans Correctional Institutions. Red had a reputation, both out in the streets and behind the walls, for being an authentic street nigga.

Then there was Derek from City Heights. Derek had done a 36 month bid when he was fifteen at John G, a juvenile facility in Columbia, for killing a nigga at that very same park about eight years before. The beef was over some bullshit but when you were young, trying to get a reputation, and didn't give a fuck, it really didn't take much to squeeze that trigger. Derek had opened fire on a nigga with an AK-47. So young he was barely able to control the assault rifle, he shot a dude up at point blank range. The other dude never had a chance. If not for his age at the time of the offense, Derek would have likely been given a life sentence, and spent the rest of his years locked in a maximum security hole somewhere.

And then there was this nigga named Fat Mack from City View. Fat Mack was a fat, black, ugly mothafucka with a lazy eye, and he had a stable full of bad bitches that would "put that money in his pocket like a rocket!" Nobody could understand how this fat, ugly ass nigga kept those quarter bitches on his team in check.

Whenever somebody on the outside looking in would pose the question as to how Fat Mack kept so many hoes breaking off that bread for him, he'd simply laugh, and say some fly shit like, "Nigga, either you pimpin' or you simpin'. It was my fuckin' destiny to live a pimp legacy! And I'd advise all you niggas to go get you a bottle of Heinz, 'cause it's gonna be a minute befo' y'all "catch up" to *any* pimpin' of mines!"

The list of hood stars and local celebrities present at Cleveland Park that Sunday went on and on. There was even a rumor that Kevin Garnett, who was originally from the Mauldin section of Greenville, might come through and show some love.

The potential for violence was always present when there were that many egos and 'hood niggas in the same place at the same time, but for the most part everybody was just chilling. People were enjoying the weather and the overall atmosphere. There were even a few people cranking the grills up to barbeque. A few scuffles broke out here and there, but nothing that serious.

The 'hood rats and gold diggers were also out in full force. They were wearing bikinis and short shorts that were all in the cracks of their hot asses, leaving little to the imagination of anybody who looked. They were competing with one another, trying to catch the attention of the young ballers, hoping to be elevated to that coveted role of wifey so they could experience what life was like in the fast lane. At least for however long the nigga they got with had their run, and stayed his ass outta jail. It could be a few years, months, or even weeks before those same niggas they were chasing behind were being chased by an indictment.

One of the most notable gold diggers on the scene that day was a girl named Abby. Abby was a straight schemer. Over the years, she'd set numerous niggas up for her boyfriends, and had even allowed them to rob places where she was employed. Her nickname in the street was Scams because there wasn't a scam in the book she hadn't tried. Everything from claiming kids that weren't hers on her income taxes, to having kinky sex with her boss, taping it, and then using the tape to blackmail him for cash. She was a high yellow broad with hazel eyes, and a nice shape, but she was beginning to show signs of wear and tear. That's what came along with the life of jumping from one hustler's dick to another, and having unprotected sex with them. Abby had A.I.D.S. and knew it, but continued to recklessly suck and fuck niggas like it was nothing but a mild cold. She had infected lots of them with the deadly disease. Some nigga had given it to her, so she felt no remorse in returning the favor. She took the term "pay it forward" to another level. The dudes she infected would then turn around and have sex with their wives, girlfriends, and in some cases, men, steadily passing the disease along. And people wondered why A.I.D.S. had become an epidemic of such proportions in the Black community. Some mothafuckas were so ignorant.

$$$

There was a two way street that ran along side of the park. That was the strip, where niggas drove by as slow as possible, to make sure everybody got a good look at their candy painted box Chevy's, Bubbles, and Donks sitting high on 26's, 28's, and even 30 inch rims.

At six o'clock, Ant D and Mike came through in Ant's new '07 drop top, flip flop Corvette, and the game was officially over. The Vette was sitting on 21 inch chrome Giovanni rims in the back, and 20 inch Giovanni's in the front, which gave it a mean stance. The rims were wrapped in low profile Pirelli tires. Nobody could really tell what color the car was because, depending on the angle you looked at it from, it appeared to be yellow, orange, or a light green hue.

Muh'fuckas were catching whiplash trying to peep the Vette, and the two young, fly ass niggas in it. Ant D pressed the play button on his iPod, which was hooked up to the stereo system in the car. Jeezy's voice came blasting out of the speakers, and the trunk sounded like King Kong was in that mothafucka trying to get out!

"I'm a T-R-A-P S-T-A-R, got the city on lock, big shoes on the car, and she likes it…she likes it, she likes it…aayyyy!"

Ant turned the volume up even louder, acknowledging the hateful and envious stares that came from the crowd of spectators. The women were practically drooling and slobbering, like kids in the window of one of those little yellow school buses.

Ant and Mike knew niggas were hating from the sidelines, but fuck that. They came there to shine until they blinded muh'fuckas. And if somebody was stupid enough to try some dumb shit, they had a stash box in the car with two newly purchased, fully loaded pistols in it.

Ant pulled into the parking lot slowly. He was looking for a space to park but the lot was jam packed. Finally, Mike peeped somebody backing out of a spot. He got Ant's attention, who then pulled into the parking space, and killed the ignition.

"Man, I can't even believe this bullshit. Them hoes from the club wore my ass out last night, dog," said Mike.

"Nigga, you ain't playing. I ain't never bust that many times in one night befo'. I thought I was gonna have to pop one of them lil' blue smurfs to keep up wit' them bitches," Ant D laughed, referring to Viagra.

"Man, that little bitch Angel was a straight mutt, my nigga! I'm talkin' 'bout she was doin' all that shit them porn stars be doin' in them videos! I ain't showed you the flicks?"

"Hell naw, you ain't show me no pictures. Nigga, you was too busy tryna choke them bitches to death to show me any pictures," Ant said, laughing and thinking back on that crazy ass scene from the hotel.

"Anyway, where they at?"

Mike looked confused. "Where what at?"

"The pictures you took, nigga!"

Mike reached into his pocket and pulled out his cell. He went to the menu and clicked on the pictures. Just then, images of Angel with a face full of sperm came onto the small color screen. He handed the phone to his friend, and let him check it out. There were shots of Diamond kissing Chocolate, and them eating each other out. There were also shots of Diamond kissing both Chocolate and Angel. But when Ant got to the pictures of Angel blowing bubbles with the cum in her mouth, he went fool.

"Oh shit! Ooooooh shit! I knew I should'a kept that bitch Angel in the room with me, dog! This bitch is a straight animal."

"What I tell you, nigga, huh?! You thought I was lyin'? That shit was crazy last night!"

They continued to reminisce animatedly on the previous nights' sexual exploits without the thought ever crossing their minds that they had failed to use protection. Who wanted to think about catching a disease, and let alone talk about it, after a night of raw, nasty sex? Niggas tended to put shit like that out of their minds because they thought it couldn't happen to them. But sometimes the price of one night of indiscretion could cost a person a lot more than they were willing to pay.

"Nigga, you see how them hoes was showin' out?"

"Yeah, I see, nigga. I ain't blind." Ant D opened his car door, which went up like the doors on a Lamborghini. He tossed the phone back to Mike. "Come on nigga, let's see who all out this bitch."

"That's what it is," said Mike, as he opened the passenger side door and got out. As he was getting out of the car, he happened to glance to his left, and saw a group of four girls walking together. One of them was a girl by the name of Nikki Jones, who Mike used to go to Greenville High School with before he had dropped out a few years back. Mike had always wanted to holler at her, but back then he was just a nobody ass nigga, still committing petty crimes and getting kicked out of school every other week for fighting, and other bullshit. She used to be a cheerleader, and one of the smartest girls in the school. So Mike would often check her out from a distance when they were in class together, but he never got up the nerve to approach her. Today would be different though.

"A yo, Ant, peep this here, my nigga. I just seen somebody I ain't seen in a lil' minute. I'm finna go holla at her real quick. I'll get up wit' you at the ball court."

"Bet it up." They gave each other quick pounds, and Ant D walked off towards the basketball court, which was on the other side of the park.

Mike approached the group of girls. "Excuse me for bothering y'all, but ain't your name Nikki," he asked, looking at the light skinned girl with the natural green eyes.

"Yes, my name is Nikki. Do I know you?"

"Naw, you don't really know me like that, but my name is Mike. We used to go to Greenville together."

"Oh yeah, I remember you now," she said, with a slight smirk on her face. "You were the one who used to be fighting all the time, getting suspended."

"Yeah, that was me," said Mike, laughing. He was surprised that she even remembered him.

"Oh, my bad, Mike. These are my homegirls, Brandy, Vicki, and Nique."

"What's up y'all, what's 'hood?"

"Nothing much, just out here chillin', and enjoying this good weather," replied Brandy.

"Who was that dude that got out of the car with you? And was it his?" asked Vicki, like the true gold-digger she was.

"Oh yeah, that was my dog, Ant D. And of course that was his shit! We ain't finna be ridin' 'round in nobody else shit like that."

"Damn, where he went to?! I need to find his sexy ass! And he got money too?!"

"Ummm Mike, you've got to excuse my friend. She gets like that sometimes," Nikki stated, looking pointedly at her friend. She was obviously embarrassed by Vicki's comments.

"What?" Vicki asked innocently. "I can't help it if I'm attracted to niggas wit' paper. I damn sho' don't want no broke ass nigga that's still livin' wit' his mama!"

"Like I said, Mike, you've got to excuse my homegirl."

"That ain't nothin'. I ain't even really sweatin' that right there. But if you don't mind, Nikki, can I holla' at you for a minute by yourself?"

"Sure, what's up Mike?" Nikki asked, walking away from her friends with him.

After a short distance, Mike turned to Nikki and said, "Nikki, would it be a problem if I got yo' number, so I can call and rap wit' you for a minute?"

Nikki didn't answer him at first, which had Mike thinking that either she hadn't heard him, or was about to turn his ass down. He was getting ready to ask her again, but she replied after a few seconds. "No, that's not a problem." She gave him her number, and he saved it in his cell phone.

"What you gettin' into tonight, after you leave the park?" Mike asked her.

"To be honest with you, Brandy was trying to get me to go with them to Escalade to see Jeezy perform, but I've got some stuff to do tomorrow. So I was thinking about just going home and getting some rest. Plus, I'm not really into the whole club scene. I got some studying I need to do for some exams I got coming up at school."

"Where you goin' to school at?" Mike inquired.

"I'm in Tech. I'm getting my degree in computer programming."

"That's what's up, Nikki. I really respect a woman that's pursuing her goals like that. But do me one favor."

"It depends on what it is."

"Come out to the club tonight and chill wit' me."

"I'll think about it," Nikki said, and walked off towards her friends.

Mike stood there for a minute, just admiring the sexy way her hips moved when she walked. He hoped to see her at the club later on that night.

$$$

"Pass the ball! Pass the muh'fuckin' ball!" exclaimed the tall, dark skinned brother standing at the top of the key of the basketball court. Finally, the rock was passed to him. He immediately faked left, and then went right, leaving the nigga who was supposed to be guarding him on the ground looking stupid with a sprained ankle. He drove to the lane, jumped in the air with the ball, did a windmill, and then slammed it into the basket with as much force as possible. All of this happened within a matter of seconds.

Everybody who saw what had just gone down went fool. "Did you see that shit?!" asked one person excitedly. "Goddamn, that nigga showin' out!" exclaimed somebody else.

"Yo Shawn, I think you broke that nigga's ankle on that one there, homey!" exclaimed Ant D.

"Naw, I just shook his ass outta them fake ass J's he got on.

Muh'fucka should know better than to be guarding me when the jump man is missing off one of them shits," replied Shawn, referring to the imitation Jordans his latest victim was wearing. "The muh'fuckin' jump man missin' the ball *and* the hand!"

The crowd broke out laughing. Shawn McGee was a tall, dark skinned, lanky dude from Piedmont Manor. He went to Southside High School, and was the starting forward on the varsity basketball team. He had taken them to the 3A championship games the previous year. It was rumored that several colleges were looking to recruit him. Basketball was his life. Every day you'd catch him in the gym after school, practicing like he was possessed. And every weekend you'd catch him at the park putting on a show for the people.

"Fuck that! Since y'all niggas slobberin' all over Shawn dick like a bunch of bitches, I got five stacks, cash money, that say my lil' brother and two mo' niggas will beat the shit outta Shawn and any two niggas stupid enough to ride wit' him," yelled Nut from the sidelines. He pulled out fifty crisp one hundred dollar bills wrapped in a rubber band.

"Shiiiiiiiit, nigga, you ain't said nothin' but a word," replied Ant D. He pulled out a stack of his own money.

"Then it's a bet. Let Stacey hold the money," said Nut, referring to a girl from Berea who was standing on the sideline. They each gave Stacey their five thousand dollars to hold. She stuffed both the stacks of bills into her bra.

Shawn picked two young ballers that he knew were decent to run with him, and Adrian, Nut's little brother, picked his two. Adrian was 5'8", and had serious game despite his height. He was like a smaller version of A.I. He was small, but fearless when it came to going to the hole. And his handle was sicker than a muh'fucka with the flu!

The game was going to 11 - you make it you take it. If both teams had point game, they had to win by 2. The game started out going back and forth, with no team really dominating the other. The score was tied at 5, but all of a sudden, Adrian took over and scored four consecutive shots. Three penetrating lay-ups, and one jump shot that was so sweet it didn't even touch the net going in.

"That's what the fuck I'm talkin' 'bout! I told y'all my lil' brother was the fuckin' truth!" exclaimed Nut. "You might as well give me my money now!"

"Come on, Shawn, tighten that shit up," encouraged Ant D.

"I got this," replied Shawn.

The score was 9 to 5, and Adrian had the ball again, driving to the lane. He went up for a lay-up, and Shawn came flying out of nowhere. He knocked the ball forcefully out of the air, and into the hands of his teammate, who immediately took the open shot and made it.

After that, Shawn went to work. They tried to double him when he came inside, but he just made them pay with one acrobatic shot after another. After putting in four baskets of his own, the score was now point game to 9, in favor of Shawn and his squad. Shawn had the ball at the wing. He was so feared from that spot, Adrian got out of position and ran over to help, leaving his man wide open. Shawn started to drive baseline, but then at the last second made a no look pass to his teammate, who made a jump shot off the backboard. Game over!

The crowd went crazy screaming and yelling. Nobody had really thought Shawn and them could come back after the way Adrian had been scoring.

"Fuck that! This shit ain't over yet. I want some get back," yelled Nut. "If I can't get no get back, then you ain't gettin' paid!" He said, reneging on the initial bet.

"Fuck you mean I ain't gettin' paid," fumed Ant D. He walked over to where Stacey was to get his money.

"Exactly what the *fuck* I said, nigga! I ain't stutter, bitch," replied Nut. He pulled a black Glock 9mm from his waist, and let it hang down by his side. "Now… can I get some mothafuckin' get back, or what?!"

All of a sudden from Nut's blindside, he was hit with a savage two-piece. The blows to his face caused him to stagger, and his gun fell to the pavement, and went off in the process.

The loud gunshot made people scatter away from the ball court, including Stacey, who was now 10 G's richer. They were trying to get the fuck out of there before the police showed up, or they got hit with a stray bullet.

But unfortunately, somebody was already hit when Nut's gun inadvertently went off. It was Shawn. He lay prone on the pavement with a hole in his chest. Blood was seeping out of the wound. His homey Trap saw his boy on the ground bleeding, and tried to get somebody's attention to get some help or call for an ambulance. But amidst all of the chaos, his pleas fell on deaf ears. Trap couldn't do anything but hold his friend in his arms as his life slowly drained from his body.

"Come on, Shawn, you too strong to die, nigga. You still got too much to do. Too much to live for, nigga. You gon' be the one who make it out for us, man… Come on, man! Hold on, dog…"

Trap was already talking to a corpse. Shawn died in his friend's arms, right along with any promising future that he might've had. Trap held his homey in his arms, and despite him trying to be a strong about the situation, the tears still somehow managed to escape from his eyes. Another dream permanently deferred, for no good reason. That seemed to happen too frequently in the 'hood.

"See, that's why I hate coming out here," said one girl. "It always be some bullshit."

"Girl, you ain't *never* lied. Somebody always wanna start some shit. Everybody was out here having a good time, and then all of a sudden, them niggas start that crazy shit."

Back on the basketball court, there was a riot going on. The nigga who had stole on Nut was from the District, so even though Nut was in the wrong, other niggas from his 'hood jumped in. Even a few gangsta ass bitches from West G helped him.

Nut reached down to pick up his pistol, but was savagely kicked in the face by somebody rocking some all white retro '92 Jordan's.

The melee went on for several minutes until the inevitable happened. The flashing blue lights of police cars could be seen. The pigs were coming down the road about five cars deep.

Niggas started getting light. Damn near everybody out there ran because they had warrants on them, or were wanted for questioning in open cases. The few that weren't didn't want to spend the rest of the afternoon answering questions from some redneck Greenville County police. So the brawl quickly turned into a track meet, with niggas running the 40 yard dash like they were trying out for the NFL!

Ant D and Mike met back up at the Corvette, and they both hopped in. Before he started up the car, Ant turned to Mike and asked if he had seen Meka anywhere out there at the park.

"Naw, I ain't seen her the whole day," answered Mike, still breathing heavily from the run to the car.

"That's strange," said Ant D. "I ain't never known Meka to miss the park on Sundays."

"Man, ain't no tellin' where Meka crazy ass is at, dog."

"Yeah, you right. Ain't no tellin'," stated Ant D, as he started the car up and screeched off into the late afternoon.

Chapter 14

"First I'm gon' stack my dough!"

"And then what," the crowd yelled.

"Then I'm gon' stack some mo'!"

"And then what?" The crowd yelled again.

"Fall back in the cut so I can do my count - hide the rest of the yams at my aunty house!"

Young Jeezy was on stage at the very packed Club Escalade, performing hits from his classic first album, "Let's Get It: Thug Motivation 101". The club had been open since nine, but Jeezy didn't get on stage until about midnight. And now muh'fuckas were losing their minds and voices, rapping along with Jeezy, word for word.

Everybody except for Mike. After that shit had gone down at the park, Ant D had dropped him off at one of his spots in Augusta Hills, so he could change and get right for the show. Once inside the apartment, Mike had took a hot shower and put on some fresh swag. For some reason, the possibility of seeing Nikki was the only thing on his mind. Mike was never one to be on that Ne-Yo, Bobby Valentino, R&B shit when it came to the ladies, but with Nikki it was different somehow. He wanted a chance to get to know her better. She was just so different from the regular cheddar chasing 'hood rats he was used to fucking with.

So now that he was at the club, all he could think about was seeing her beautiful face again. Mike walked over to the bar and posted up, observing the crowd.

Thirty minutes later, he felt like a fool. Just when he was about to say fuck it, and go enjoy the show, Nikki walked through the doors of the packed club, and made her way over to the bar where he was standing.

"Hey Mike," she said.

For a moment Mike was so caught up in how beautiful she looked, he couldn't even speak.

Nikki was wearing a tight dress that showed off her curves, but didn't look nasty and show too much. She was 5'8", but the heels she wore pushed her up to about 5'11". She stood damn near eye to eye with Mike, who was 6 feet tall.

Almost thirty seconds passed, and Mike still hadn't said anything. Nikki jokingly asked him, "What's wrong, Mike, you don't like my dress, or somethin'?"

Finally Mike came to his senses, and replied, "Nikki, I know this is gon' sound real corny but it's real. Your beauty kinda' left me speechless. I saw you, and was like DAMN! I couldn't say shit," he said, smiling and showing a mouth full of diamonds and rubies.

"Thank you, Mike. That was sweet. How long have you been here?"

"Too long," he responded.

"I thought you liked Jeezy."

"I do. But honestly, I didn't come out here to see the Snowman."

"Then who did you come to see?"

Mike looked in her eyes, and said, "You. Look, Nikki, I don't like wasting time so I'ma just say what's on my mind. I know we barely know each other, but I wanna change all of that, if you'll let me."

"Mike, I've heard a lot about you already, and I'm not trying to be just another one of your hoes. Somebody you just have sex with. So maybe it would be better if we were just friends."

"Damn, Nikki. I see you done did your homework on a nigga," said Mike, grinning. "Look, I know I have a reputation when it comes to dealin' with girls, but you gotta understand that I only treat women like that if they allow me to. I don't respect them. Not the easy ones. I respect you. You're smart, you're beautiful, and you got goals. You tryna do something with your life. All I'm tryna do is get to know you better, and hopefully become a part of that life. Matter fact, let's get up outta this noisy ass club, and go somewhere where we can talk."

"Well, it looks like we both did our homework," Nikki stated. "Alright, Mike. But understand that all we're going to do is go talk. So if you have anything else on your mind, then we might as well not even leave."

"Like I said, Nikki, I respect you. And with that respect comes my word that I'll never do anything that you don't want me to," Mike said, extending his hand to her. She took it, and he lifted her hand to his lips and kissed it. Together, they turned and headed for the exit.

"*When they hear that new Jeezy all the dope boys go crazy, all the dope boys go crazy! I pop my collar then I swing my chain, you can catch me in the club pimpin' doin' my thang...*"

It was a ten minutes to one A.M. and Young Jeezy was still on stage. He was sweating from giving the crowd their money's worth, enthused on each song that he performed. All of the women at the front of the stage were grabbing at Jeezy's pants and crotch, trying to get his attention. They damn near pulled him off the stage. The crowd continued to rap along. It was safe to say that the 'hoods of Upstate South Carolina had love for him.

Several other rap artists had already come to different clubs in the UPS that year, but had ended up getting shit thrown at them while they were on stage. A few of those same rappers were even shot at, or relieved of their cash and jewelry at gunpoint. But niggas felt like Jeezy was one of them.

Ant D was upstairs at a table overlooking the crowd, enjoying the view with two thick ass women from Spartanburg, S.C. at the table with him. He had two bottles of Moet sitting in a large bucket of ice, and was smoking on a blunt so fat it was obese.

Jeezy's last song, "Soul Survivor", was the one Ant D had waited all night to hear. *"Let's get it! If you lookin' for me I'll be on the block wit' that thing cocked, possibly sittin' on a drop now. 'Cause Im'a rider, yeeeeeah, soul survivor, yeeeeeeeeah. Everybody know the game don't stop, tryna make it to the top befo' ya' ass get popped now - If you a rider, yeeeeeeea, a soul survivor..."*

Ant D jumped up onto the table with a bottle of Moet in each hand, and the blunt still lit in his mouth. He did a little two step on the table, closed his eyes, and felt the best he'd ever felt in his whole entire twenty years on the face of the earth. He had money to blow, bad bitches to fuck, and the best weed to smoke. And not to mention the finest fishscale to snort. What else could a 'hood nigga from the gutter, who never had shit coming up, ask for?

And they were just getting started. It was only a matter of time before him and Mike made themselves certified 'hood stars. Once they made a few more licks, he'd make sure his mama and Meka were set up straight. *And where the fuck was Meka at anyway*, Ant thought to himself momentarily. But then the weed smoke and alcohol kicked back in and dulled his senses. He continued to enjoy the show, and reveled in his newfound ghetto celebrity status.

$$$

While Ant D was at Club Escalade partying, and having a good time, Mike was cruising in his new customized Escalade. He brought the truck to a stop in the parking lot of Falls Park. Falls Park was a beautiful spot in Downtown Greenville that had a bridge with a breathtaking view of a waterfall.

Mike got out of the truck. When he saw Nikki about to open the passenger door, he stopped her and said, "Naw, let me get that for you, beautiful."

She smiled at the thought of Mike being such a gentleman. After all the things she'd heard about him and his reputation, the last thing she expected was for him to be opening doors for her. It was a pleasant surprise.

He walked over to her side, opened the door, and helped her step down. They walked over to the bridge that overlooked the waterfall. Even though it was early morning, the lights on the bridge illuminated a breathtaking view.

Once they reached the middle of the bridge, Nikki took off her heels. Her feet were killing her, so she was happy to be out of her shoes. Her perfectly pedicured feet felt like they were in heaven the minute they touched the cool pavement.

Mike said, "Let's stop here, and chill for a minute." They stood there shoulder to shoulder on the bridge staring up at the stars, and listening to the waterfall speaking its own sensual language.

Still gazing at the stars, Mike said, "Nikki, you got a man?"

"No," she answered softly.

"I'm not sayin' you lyin' or nothin', but damn, that's kinda' hard to believe. As pretty and smart as you is, I know niggas be comin' at you left and right."

"Yeah, but maybe the *right* one hasn't come at me yet."

Mike turned his head and took in Nikki's beautiful profile, which was illuminated by the moonlight. "Nikki, look at me." She turned and looked directly into Mike's eyes.

He continued, "Honestly, this ain't even my style right here. I'm the last nigga on the face of the earth that you would consider a romantic dude, but for some reason you make a nigga wanna do shit like this. Nikki, you're special…"

"You trying to say I'm retarded or something, Mike," Nikki joked.

"Naw, what I'm saying is that a girl like you don't come along too often, so I want you in my life. I been wantin' to holla at you since high school, but I wasn't in a position to back then."

"What do you mean you weren't in a position?"

"What I mean is that back then I was just a lil' nobody, broke ass nigga."

"Mike, everybody is not like my friend Vicki - trying to get with brothers for what they have. I mean, I like nice things and all that, but I'd rather be with someone who was broke, as long as he was working towards something better, and treated me right."

"Naw, Nikki, I didn't mean it like that. I know you ain't a gold-digger, but at the same time, a woman like you deserves to have flowers, nice dinners, jewelry... Back then I couldn't do that for you."

"And now you can?"

"Damn right."

"How Mike?"

Mike turned and stared at the waterfall for a few seconds, contemplating just how much of himself he wanted to expose. But he'd already jumped out of the window by telling her how he felt. It was too late to ask for a parachute now. After moments of serious thought, he made up his mind. "Nikki, you remember when I told you that I respect you, right?

"Yeah."

"Well, that means that I'm not gonna lie to you. I'm in the streets real heavy right now. Doin' what I gotta do to make it. And none of it's legal."

"Mike, I'm not in the streets like you but I'm not totally naïve. I know a little bit about what's going on out there. Just say for a second, hypothetically of course, that you were my man. What if something happened to you? What if you got killed, or sent to prison? I don't want to invest myself emotionally, and then... That would crush me, Mike. That's why I told myself I'd never date a guy like you. I'm not prepared for that type of pain."

"See that's the thang, Nikki. I'm not gonna be in these streets forever!" Mike said passionately. "I know this shit can't last forever. As soon as the money gets right, me and my homey Ant gettin' outta this shit."

"Mike, that's what everybody says..."

"Nikki, I'm not everybody."

She looked at Mike, her green eyes searching his face for the truth. She wanted to believe him, but couldn't hand over her heart to him and have it broken into tiny little pieces. Mike stared back at her, and wondered how he could feel so strongly about a woman so soon. Suddenly Nikki leaned towards him and closed her eyes. Mike leaned in and kissed her slowly but passionately. His tongue explored the inside of her mouth, loving the way she tasted. After kissing like that for about a minute, Nikki pulled away.

"I hope that means yes," said Mike.

"No, that's the kiss I give to men right before I turn them down," she said, laughing. "It's late, Mike. Take me home so I can do a little studying, and get some sleep."

Together, they ambled back to the truck. Twenty minutes later, Mike was pulling into an apartment complex in Berea, where Nikki stayed with her mama and little brother. They got out and walked over to apartment number 37A. Once at the door, Nikki turned around and said, "Call me tomorrow, okay?"

Mike nodded yes, and then pulled Nikki in closer and tried to kiss her again.

She pulled away from him, and said, "Tomorrow, Mike. Call me tomorrow."

Reluctantly, he respected her wishes and let her go inside of the apartment. The taste of her soft, luscious lips lingered in his mouth as he walked back to his vehicle. He felt better than he'd felt in a long time. Mike got in, and pulled off into the early morning.

Chapter 15

BEEEEP! BEEEEP! BEEEEP! The sound of the garbage truck backing up to the dumpster broke the silence and the serenity of the early Monday morning. "A little mo', Joe! Back it up a little mo'," the White, heavyset garbage man yelled to his partner in the truck. "A little mo', and you got it."

The truck inched further back, connecting with a dark green dumpster. "Alright, go ahead and lift it!"

The dumpster jerked upwards, and when it did, one of the trash bags moved, exposing what appeared to be a hand. "Hold it, Joe, hold it! I think I see something in there," the man yelled.

The dumpster stopped moving, suspended in mid-air. The garbage man leaned inside the dumpster and began to throw black trash bags out of the way with his heavily gloved hands, until he revealed the body of a naked, badly beaten, Black woman.

"Holy shit, Joe! There's a goddamn body in here, bo! Call 911!" The garbage man who'd just discovered the body turned to his side. His face beet red, he let the bacon, eggs, and toast he'd just eaten for breakfast hit the ground.

Because of the nature of the call to 911, an ambulance was dispatched to the scene, along with the closest available police unit. Once on the scene, the paramedics' main concern was to determine whether or not the woman was still alive. If so, they were focused on saving her life if they could. Unlike the police, who were busy securing the scene, and looking for any possible evidence to what appeared to be a homicide.

One of the paramedics was a pretty brunette. She reached her gloved hand into the dumpster and placed two fingers on the Jane Doe's neck. "We got a pulse! It's faint, but it's there. We've got to get her out of here, and to a hospital! Fast!"

With help from the police officers, the paramedics slowly lifted the body out of the filthy dumpster. They placed the woman on the stretcher, and into the waiting ambulance. The driver hit the siren and the emergency lights, and sped away to the nearest hospital, which was Greenville Memorial.

Once at the hospital, the trauma unit medical staff did everything within their power to keep the young woman alive, which was no small feat in the condition she was in. But with some of the best medical attention the state of South Carolina had to offer, the young woman's life was saved. Though she remained in a coma from the severe head trauma she'd sustained.

Detective Daniel Patterson walked into the intensive care unit at Memorial Hospital, where the newly admitted Jane Doe was being held. He looked around the room at all of the equipment which was being used to keep the woman alive. She had tubes in her mouth and both of her nostrils, not to mention the machine that was breathing for her.

Detective Patterson was a slightly overweight red neck with stained teeth, bad breath, and a raspy voice that he'd acquired over the years from the numerous packs of Marlboros that he smoked daily. He'd been with the department now for over 20 years, and had pretty much seen and heard it all.

Patterson stood at the foot of the bed and took in the sight of the young woman lying motionless on the hospital bed. But for some reason, the savageness of the crime didn't seem to bother him. "Probably another goddamn Black crack whore," the detective said to himself. "Seems like their asses gettin' younger and younger."

What he saw in front of him was not a defenseless, badly beaten human being that deserved empathy. Instead he saw a prime opportunity that he planned to take full advantage of. He was determined to find out exactly who the animals responsible for that atrocious act were, and bring the perpetrators to justice. Then hopefully they would spend the rest of their worthless lives rotting in a cell somewhere. Not because he cared anything about the young Black girl lying in front of him comatose in the hospital bed, but because he wanted that promotion to captain that had eluded him for so many years. As far as he was concerned, the Black bitch had gotten what she deserved. But that was just the type of case he needed to solve to rise in the ranks! He could see the headlines all over the news already: *"Detective Daniel Patterson heroically solves gruesome crime and is promoted to Captain."*

It was probably some more dumb, cracked out niggers who did it, so finding them should be easy. But before he could do that, he had to first find out exactly who the little young Black whore was. He walked over to her bed and began fingerprinting her left hand. Since she was Black, and more than likely a prostitute, Patterson reasoned that she had probably been picked up at some point in time.

Shit, most of these goddamn niggers got some type of fucking record somewhere anyway, thought Detective Patterson. If she had a record then the department would have her prints on file, which would save him a lot of time in trying to determine who she was.

After fingerprinting her right hand, Detective Patterson contemplated taking some pictures of the woman's face to also possibly aid him in identifying who she was. But he immediately dismissed the idea. The whore's face was so badly disfigured and swollen, any picture he took of her right then wouldn't even come close to resembling what she normally looked like. So instead he headed back to the department, and hoped that he'd have some luck with the prints.

Once back at the department, Detective Patterson turned the prints into forensics, and was told that it would be about thirty minutes to an hour before they had anything for him. That was a lot less time than it took back when he had first started on the force. Due to the new technology of having every criminal's prints in a statewide database, it made it possible for a tedious process that would have taken weeks twenty years ago to now be completed within an hour.

Detective Patterson took the opportunity to grab himself a much needed cup of coffee to help wake him up. It looked like it was going to be a long Monday, so he made his coffee cowboy style, which was straight black. He walked down the hall and lit up one of his Marlboros, ignoring the NO SMOKING signs that were posted throughout the hallway.

Twenty minutes later, he got a call from the forensics department. "Patterson, those prints you gave us a little while ago? We've got a match. Her name is Tameka Davis, 20 years of age. She was arrested on July the 4th outside of a night club for disorderly conduct and resisting arrest."

"You got an address and telephone number on her?"

"Yeah, hold on a sec," said the forensic specialist, as he scanned the computer for the additional information. "We've got a number, but no address in the system."

"Alright, let me get the number."

The specialist recited the seven digits, and Patterson jotted down the pertinent information in his spiral notepad. He wrote the number, along with the girl's name, and what she'd been arrested for. Unfortunately that's all he had for the time being.

Back in his office, Patterson dialed the number he'd been given. After several rings, somebody finally answered.

"Hello," said a tired, disoriented female's voice.

"Uh, yes ma'am, I'm trying to get in contact with a Ms. Davis?" said Patterson in his rough, gravely voice.

"Look, it's too early in the goddamn morning for you people to be calling my house with this bullshit harassing me! I told y'all muh'fuckas when I get the money..."

"Look, Ms. Davis," said Patterson, cutting her off in the middle of her tirade. "I'm not a bill collector." *Goddamn, people think everybody calling their house is a bill collector,* thought Patterson. "My name is Detective Daniel Patterson, from the Greenville County Sheriff's Department. Do you have a daughter by the name of Tameka?"

Gloria immediately sensed that something was amiss. She sat up in her bed and gripped the phone tightly. "Yeah, my daughter's name is Tameka, why? What's wrong? Is she in some type of trouble? Is she alright?"

Patterson hesitated for a second, trying to get his words together.

In the silence Gloria began to panic. "Officer, is my daughter alright?!"

Patterson cleared his throat. "Ms. Davis, your daughter is alive, but she's been beaten up pretty badly, and she sustained severe head trauma. At approximately 6:30 A.M. we received a call from a Greenville County garbage man, who said that he'd discovered a body in a dumpster that was on his route. An ambulance was dispatched to the scene along with some officers to investigate. Once it was determined that she was still alive, your daughter was transported to Memorial Hospital, where she was treated, and is currently being held in ICU." Patterson relayed all of this information without any type of compassion or regards for the effect his words might have on Gloria.

"How do you know it's my Tameka," asked Gloria, hoping that maybe this had happened to somebody else's daughter, and not hers.

The detective told her how he had fingerprinted Meka, and that the computer showed that she'd been arrested back on the 4th of July. He explained that based on that arrest, he was able to ascertain her identity and phone number.

Gloria's worse fears were confirmed. She knew it was her baby girl because she was the one who bailed Meka out the morning after that incident at the club back in July.

Not wanting to hear anymore secondhand information, Gloria

abruptly hung up the phone on the detective while he was still talking. She hurriedly threw on some clothes. Without even bothering to brush her teeth or wash her face, she ran outside to Meka's Chrysler 300c, jumped in, and screeched off towards the hospital.

Chapter 16

Ant D awoke Monday morning with a thick, brown skinned PYT's juicy lips wrapped around his dick, slowly sucking him off. After Jeezy performed at the club the night before, he left with those two freaks from Spartanburg who'd been upstairs at the table with him. They had jumped into the Vette and broke out. Since it was only a two-seater, one of the girls had to sit in the other's lap while he drunkenly swerved in and out of lanes on his way downtown to the Marriott.

He'd had every intention on fucking the shit out of both of them as soon as they got to the room, but his body had plans of its own. As soon as he walked through the door, he fell face first onto the bed and passed out. The combination of liquor, coke, and exotic weed he'd been consuming all night finally caught up with him and left him incapacitated.

While Ant was unconscious, the two girls began taking off his clothes until he was lying on the bed completely naked. Then they took turns kissing and licking all over his body, in an attempt to wake him up. Seeing that he was completely out of it, the two girls discussed whether or not to rob Ant, but they decided against it. Instead they spent the rest of the night and early morning kissing, licking, and sucking on each other until they came, and fell asleep in each other's arms.

The hot, wet sensation of the girl's mouth working up and down and back and forth on his dick was enough to finally bring Ant D out of his slumber. He opened his eyes and glanced at the brown skinned freak that was on her knees between his legs with her thick lips locked around his meat. He couldn't remember her name, but her head game was sick enough to give Karrine "Superhead" Steffans a run for her money.

When she noticed that he was awake and looking at her, she took his erect penis out of her mouth and kissed the head affectionately. She acted like there was absolutely nothing on the earth she'd rather be doing than sucking on his dick.

Her homegirl, who was lying beside Ant D completely naked, pulled her legs back and began rubbing on her own pussy while she watched her friend give him head. The first girl took Ant's cock all the way down her throat, until her nose was buried in his pubic hairs. All the while she kept her eyes locked on his. She gagged and pulled her mouth off of Ant's dick, and left slobber and spit all over it. She spit on his dick again, and used that lubrication to work his rock hard shaft back and forth with her hand.

After a few minutes of the freak giving him head, Ant couldn't hold back any longer. He closed his eyes, curled his toes, and violently let go inside of the girl's steaming, waiting mouth, while gripping her head with both hands. She swallowed every single drop of his cum like it was her favorite flavored milkshake.

Just then, the new Lil' Scrappy ring tone went off on Ant's phone. *"I got money in the bank – shawty, what you thank? I got money in the bank, shawty, what you thank?"*

Ant D leaned over the side of the bed in order to retrieve his phone out of his jeans. Once he got it out, he flipped it open and said, "Yeah?"

"Anthony?!!" The shrill sound of his mama's voice calling him by his full birth name got Ant D's attention immediately. The only time she ever called him Anthony was when shit was seriously wrong. He swung his legs over the side of the bed and sat up, bracing himself for whatever was coming.

"Yeah mama, what's up?"

"They got Meka! Somebody tried to kill Meka! The police done called. They found her in the trash," screamed Gloria incoherently. She kept talking, but she was speaking so fast and loud that Ant only caught bits and pieces of what she said.

"Hold up, mama, hold up! Slow down. I can't understand what you sayin' with you talkin' all fast like that. Calm down so I can understand you."

Gloria took a deep breath and spoke as calmly as she could, given the circumstances. She said, "Somebody tried to kill Meka. A detective called me a few hours ago. They found her in a…in a…dumpster." Gloria broke down sobbing.

"Where they got her at now, mama?"

"Greenville Memorial."

Ant pressed the end button on his phone, jumped up from the bed, and began getting dressed.

"What's wrong, baby," asked the girl who'd just finished swallowing his unborn children. She was sitting at the foot of the bed, naked, watching him get dressed.

Ant didn't even bother to answer her question. He didn't even hear her. Something had happened to Meka. He continued to get dressed, a million questions racing through his mind. After getting his last Nike on, he ran out of the hotel room down to his flip flop Corvette. He jumped in, put the key in the ignition, and left melted Pirelli rubber on the asphalt as he flew out of the parking lot on his way to the hospital.

"I don't believe that sorry ass nigga just left us in this room like this!" said one of the girls back at the hotel room.

"See, I told you we should'a went ahead and robbed that nigga while he was knocked the fuck out. *Damn!*"

Doing about 60 mph in a school zone, Ant D shifted into fourth gear and stepped on the gas, accelerating to 90 mph. He pulled his phone out and dialed Mike's number. He hadn't seen Mike since he left the club the night before, so there was no telling where he was at.

Mike answered on the fifth ring. "Hello," he said groggily.

"Man, a muh'fucka done tried to kill Meka. She in the hospital."

Mike, who was still in bed at his apartment, knew from the sound of his homey's voice that he wasn't joking. Besides, that wasn't the type of shit Ant would joke about anyway.

"What hospital she in?"

"Memorial."

"I'm on my way," said Mike, and flipped his phone shut. He rolled out of bed and started getting dressed. Before he left the apartment, Mike went to the closet in his bedroom and grabbed the AR-15, which he kept fully loaded against the back wall. He placed it in a gym bag, threw some clothes on top of it, and then headed outside to his Escalade.

Once inside the truck, Mike placed the gym bag on the floor of the passenger side. Wondering exactly what the fuck had transpired, he pulled out of his apartment complex and headed to Greenville Memorial Hospital.

Chapter 17

As soon as Ant walked through the automatic glass doors of Greenville Memorial and into the waiting area, Gloria jumped up from her seat, ran to him and began crying uncontrollably. While clinging to her son, she said, "They tried to kill my baby! Somebody tried to kill my baby girl!" Gloria placed her head on his shoulder and sobbed.

Ant D had been off the porch for a long time, and he had taken quite a few lives himself, so he refused to start that crying shit. He hadn't shed a tear since he was thirteen, and he damn sure wasn't about to start now. He needed to keep his emotions in check as much as possible in order to figure out what his next move was going to be. But he could understand his mama breaking down like that. She was after all a civilian in the war that took place daily in the inner city streets. And a war was exactly what was about to pop off behind that shit. He hugged his mother, and spoke in her ear. "Mama, you gotta calm down. We gotta be strong for Meka."

"I know, baby, I know," said Gloria. She wiped her tears, and attempted to regain her composure.

"What room they got her in? You done seen her yet?"

"Yeah, I just came out of her room right before you got here. They got her in ICU, in room number 215."

Just then, Mike walked into the waiting area with a scowl on his face. He greeted Gloria and Ant, his adopted family. "What's pop-

118

pin'?" asked Mike.

"We finna go upstairs and see her now. They got her in ICU," replied Ant D.

The three of them took off towards the elevator. Once they got in, Gloria pressed 2. ICU was located on the second floor. Once off the elevator, they walked pass a series of rooms before coming to number 215. A tall, balding, bespectacled, Caucasian man wearing a white lab coat was at the door writing on some type of chart. The man turned around as they approached. "Hello, my name's Dr. Baker. Can I help you?"

Ant D spoke up. "Yeah, we here to see Tameka Davis. Are you her doctor?"

"As a matter of fact, I am," said Dr. Baker in his nasal voice. "I was just making my rounds, checking her vital signs, and making sure that her condition hasn't worsened."

"Exactly what is her condition?" asked Mike.

"Well to be frank with you, somebody beat the crap out of her. She has severe bruising and swelling all over her face and body. A few broken ribs, and some missing teeth… And whoever the animals were that did this… also raped her. We tested her for STDs and HIV. Fortunately, everything came back negative. And as serious as all of that sounds, those are the least of our concerns right now. Due to severe trauma of the head, she remains comatose."

"Comatose? What the hell is that?" asked Ant.

"She's in a coma. And we have no way of knowing for certain if she'll even come out of it. And if she does, she may not be able to function normally."

"What do you mean *function normally*?"

"I mean even if she regains consciousness, there is a possibility… that she may never fully recover."

Gloria struggled to keep the tears fighting to come out of her eyes from sliding down her face. "Can we see her," asked Ant.

"Sure, but if y'all don't mind, only one at a time. And only for a few minutes," replied Dr. Baker, as he went back to writing on

Meka's chart.

Ant D went into the room first. He'd seen worse, and in fact had done worse to people. But seeing his twin sister, one of the only people he actually loved, lying up in that bed with tubes running through her body was enough to break even a cold hearted nigga like him down. He and Meka had been through so much together over the years. He told himself that he wasn't going to cry, and he was doing a good job until he walked over to her bed and saw what the fuck them niggas had done to her. His sister's face was beautiful, but they had her looking like Emitt Till up in that muh'fucka. Her face and head were so swollen that if not for the birthmark on her lower neck, he wouldn't have believed he looking at his own twin sister. A single tear escaped from his right eye and slowly trickled down his cheek. He grabbed Meka's hand and spoke to her, not knowing for sure if she could hear him. Deep inside, he had a feeling that she could.

There were some things he had to get off his chest. "Meka, what it is, baby girl? I really don't know what to say other than this. Yo' ass better not die on me, I know that shit. We done been through too much together, ya heard? I need for you to be a soldier, and pull through for me, so we can get them niggas that did this shit to you."

After a few seconds of intense silence, Ant said, "I…I know I don't ever tell you this shit but…I love you, Meka. Anyway, I'ma get at you later, sis. Alright?"

As Ant D turned and walked out of the room, he said to himself, "I *swear* somebody's gonna die behind this bullshit."

Chapter 18

Mike walked into the hospital room next. He sadly looked at the girl who over the past five years had become the sister he'd never had. Looking at Meka laid up in the bed like that with a ventilator breathing for her put Mike in a zone. He stood there trying to keep his emotions under control, and reflected back on his life, and the first time he'd met Meka....

Ever since the day Tracy Dillinger had given birth to Mike, he'd constantly been on the move, from one foster home to another. Tracy's parents had been too ashamed of the circumstances behind Mike's birth to take him in.

Tracy's father and Mike's grandfather, John Dillinger, was a pastor with one of the largest churches in the upstate of South Carolina. He had a strong flock of followers that were willing to follow the articulate, charismatic, young Black preacher to the end of the earth, if he led them there. But what would his congregation and the community have thought about him if they had found out that his own daughter had had unprotected sex with a man twice her age? What kind of man could lead a church, but couldn't keep his own daughter from getting pregnant before the age of 16?

So when Tracy became pregnant and told her mother, who was director of the choir, and also the Sunday school teacher, it was immediately decided that the pregnancy would remain a secret, and never be discussed outside of the house.

An abortion was out of the question though. For Pastor D, as his flock so affectionately called him, was a deeply religious man with the belief that abortion was an abomination; murder of an innocent life. So while he was very deeply concerned with his appearance in the community, he was even more concerned with his appearance before God. Therefore he wasn't willing to be an accomplice to murder, no matter how small and seemingly insignificant the life. No, Tracy would have the baby, give it up for adoption, and then the whole family would move on and learn from that terrible mistake.

All during her pregnancy, Tracy's mother, Esther, would go to clothing stores and buy her daughter clothes that were many sizes too big for her small frame, in order to conceal the fact that she was with child. If anybody asked about the clothes, Tracy was to say that she had just put on some weight. They knew it was a sin to lie, but the Dillingers looked at it as a necessary evil. It was just a little "white lie."

But it turned out that the clothes and lies weren't even necessary. Tracy was so depressed about the fact that the man who'd swore he'd never leave her was gone, she barely ate. Add that to all of the additional stress that came with trying to keep her pregnancy a secret. Three months into her first trimester, she had actually dropped a few pounds. She wasn't getting the proper nutrition for herself, let alone for her baby.

But the baby boy in her womb was a fighter who refused to be denied the opportunity to walk on this earth and kick up a little dust while he was here. Eight months into her pregnancy, Tracy prematurely gave birth to Michael Trevall Dillinger… losing her life in the process.

Pastor D and his wife immediately put the baby up for adoption, and told the congregation that Tracy had died from a rare disease that she'd been battling for months. They even went so far as to take their family name away from the baby, so know one would ever connect the dots. The changed the baby's last name to something more common, like "Smith."

The pastor and his wife were uncomfortable with the lie they were telling, but it became easier to deal with as the years went by. Though *they both severely missed their only daughter, Pastor D and his wife never spoke about their feelings. It was just a dark cloud that hovered over their lives as the years passed. Each year the memory of what had happened faded, until finally it seemed as if the whole experience had been nothing but a bad dream that was finally over. But for young Michael, the nightmare was just beginning.*

Anybody who's ever been a foster kid knew that was a lonely, insecure life to live. Oftentimes the family who took a child into their home only did so to receive the check that was allotted to them each month from the state. The child could suffer physical abuse, neglect, or both. After the child became too much of a burden, they were shipped back to DSS to be placed into another home. The older the child got, the less likely it was that they'd be permanently adopted by a family. That usually left the adolescent questioning why nobody wanted them, or why they weren't good enough.

That was Mike's reality up until the age of eleven, when he began to have frequent run-ins with the law. After numerous arrests for petty crimes, a judge sentenced Mike to spend the rest of his adolescence in the Greenville Group Home in West Greenville. He was to remain there until the age of eighteen.

The group home wasn't any different than a regular foster home to Mike. As far as he was concerned, it was the same shit, but just a different toilet that needed to be flushed. There were just a lot more castaways that nobody wanted bunched up under the same roof.

One day when Mike was fourteen, and high as a cloud from some good weed he'd smoked with his roommate Stutter Bug, he decided to walk up the road to the Cash and Carry convenience store to buy some snacks. He needed to silence the stomach rumbling caused by the good trees he'd just finished burning.

Once he got to the store, a group of teens pulled a knife on him, and tried to rob him for his brand new pair of Air Jordan's, and the little bit of cash he had in his pockets.

There were four of them against just him, but Mike was like "fuck it, let's get it poppin'!" The thought of running had never even crossed his mind. It just wasn't in him to run from a problem. He'd rather run towards it.

Just as Mike was about to steal on the kid holding the knife, a boy and a girl who very closely resembled each other walked out of the store and asked him what was going on. When Mike explained what was going down, the boy spoke up.

"Man, y'all ain't finna jump this man. If y'all wanna fight him, then give him a one on one. Y'all ain't fixin' to jump him like that."

The kids argued back and forth for a second, until the short stocky one who was holding the knife got tired of all the tongue wrestling. He took a swing at Mike with the knife. Mike sensed it coming, and jumped back to avoid the blade. He staggered off balance in the process.

Once he regained his balance, Mike hit dude with a flurry of punches that were so swift, the short stocky nigga's only option was to try to scoop Mike. He went under Mike, grabbed his legs and took him on a Six Flags ride through the air until his body slammed onto the ground. Once he was on the ground, the other kids tried to stomp Mike's face into the concrete. And that's when all hell broke loose.

The young girl who had come out of the store pulled a glass juice bottle out of her bag, and hit one of the kids in the face with it. His head split open, and the wound spurted blood. The boy screamed out in pain. The other two boys ran up on her, but the boy standing beside her, who happened to be her twin brother, started throwing haymakers at them. He was trying to knock their asses out!

His sister joined in again, swinging the glass bottle wildly, until it connected with somebody else's head. The melee went on for a few minutes, until the proprietor of the Cash and Carry called the police.

Once the police car pulled up to the scene, the group of youths immediately took off and scattered. The four who had started it ran in one direction, while Mike and the two siblings who'd helped him ran in the other. They headed down a side road.

After running until their chests were heaving from the physical exertion, Mike and the two twins slowed down and began walking at a normal pace. After catching his breath, Mike said, "Man, y'all ain't even had to do that. I was straight. I could'a handled that shit…"

"I can't tell," said the girl, laughing.

Mike laughed too. "But on some real shit, I appreciate y'all gettin' down wit' a nigga like that, fa' real."

"Ain't nothin', dog," said the boy. "I hate it when niggas be tryna put it down on muh'fuckas for no reason. And most of them niggas be pussy anyway."

"What y'all names is anyway?" asked Mike.

"My name's Ant D. This here is my twin sister, Meka," he said, pointing towards the girl on his left.

"Nigga, I can talk," said Meka sarcastically, as she playfully punched her brother in the arm. "What's your name?"

"Mike," he replied. "We gonna have to change your name though," he said to Meka jokingly.

"Change my name? Nigga, you trippin'. Change my name fo' what?"

"Because the way you was swinging that fuckin' bottle, a muh'fucka might have to start calling yo' ass Mrs. Barry Bonds, or some shit."

"Oh my God, that was lame! Was that supposed to be a joke? Because if it was, that shit was real corny," said Meka.

All three of them started laughing. From that day forth, the three of them were inseparable. At the age of fifteen, Mike ran away from the group home and began living with Ant D and Meka at their mama's house in The District…

The sound of Dr. Baker's voice interrupted Mike's reflection on the past, and brought him back to the harsh reality of the present. Somebody had tried to kill his adopted sister, and now she was in a hospital bed fighting for her life.

"Excuse me, sir. I hate to interrupt, but visiting hours are over…"

Mike looked at Meka for another second, and then silently turned and walked out of the room. He vowed to himself that whoever was responsible for that shit wouldn't just die, but they would suffer.

Chapter 19

Back downstairs in the waiting area, Ant D and Mike discussed the situation and contemplated their next move. Gloria was in the gift shop buying flowers and get-well-soon balloons to decorate Meka's room with. A few of Meka's homegirls had come through to show their support after they got the word about what had happened to her.

"Who you think did this bullshit? You think it had somethin' to do with Twan? Or just some crazy ass niggas that don't wanna live too much longer tryna get a rep?" Mike asked quietly, doing his best to not be overheard by the other people in the waiting room.

"Come on, Mike. Me and you both know that in these streets ain't no such thing as a muh'fuckin' coincidence. Everybody and they mama knew that Meka was Twan's main girl. He turns up dead, and not even two days later, Meka out at the mall shopping like she just hit the lotto."

"Yeah, yeah, I know. I tried to tell her ass shit was too hot for her to be going out buyin' up shit like that. That nigga's body - or what was left of it - wasn't even in the fuckin' urn good before she copped that Range," Mike said, frustrated.

"Shit, we both tried to get her ass to fall back, but you know how my sister do when her mind is set on somethin'. Ain't nothin' finna stop her 'til that shit gets done. And niggas ain't fuckin' slow. It don't take no muh'fuckin' rocket scientist to add all that shit up."

"Shit still don't make no sense though, Ant. If niggas know what went down, then why they ain't tried to get at *us*? It ain't like we been hard to find these last few days."

"That's the thing, Mike. Whoever them coward ass niggas was that did this shit probably ain't really sure what the fuck went down. But they figured Meka had to have something to do with it, so they snatched her up and tried to get her to put the rest of the pieces of the puzzle together for 'em."

"And knowing Meka's crazy ass, she probably bucked on them niggas!" Mike said, chuckling.

"That's off top. You know my sis a muh'fuckin' soldier, dog."

"So how we gonna find these dudes?"

"Oh, that shit ain't gon' be too hard, my nigga. You know these niggas out here can't hold no water. Especially if the price right, like Bob Barker."

"What you mean?"

Ant D scratched his chin for a second, lost in thought. After a few moments of contemplation, he said, "I'm thinkin' like this here. After all the money we blew these past few weeks, we should still be sittin' on 'bout three and some change, right? I guarantee you if we put a hundred stacks out there for word on who was behind this shit, somebody gon' sing like fuckin' Usher, or one of them other R&B niggas."

"That sounds like a good idea. I'm wit' it. And if Meka comes outta that coma before we hear somethin', then she can tell us what went down herself. Either way, once we find out what's what, we finna turn this bitch into Iraq!!" Mike was amped up at finally having a course of action to take. Retaliation was a must. Revenge was like the sweetest joy…next to getting pussy.

"In the meantime, we need to go 'head and find some artillery."

"Shiiiiiiit, you know I got the chopper fully loaded in the truck right now."

"That ain't gonna be enough though, Mike. I'm talkin' 'bout really serving these niggas. What's up wit that nigga you got that AR from? He got some mo' shit like that?"

"Stutter Bug? Damn right. I don't know how he be doin' it, but that nigga keep some heavy shit on deck. I think he got a plug out there in Fort Jackson, the military base in Columbia."

"Call that nigga up and see what's 'hood. Tell him we gon' need that heavy shit. AK's, AR's, vests - the whole throw. If we goin' to war, then ain't no point in playing wit' these fuck niggas."

"I'm wit' you on that, homey. I'm finna go to the payphone outside and call his ass now. I ain't tryna use my cell for no shit like that. I just heard that the fuckin' feds done trapped Man Man off for talkin' reckless on his cell."

"Yeah, I heard 'bout that shit too. Them crackers gettin' advanced with that slick technology shit, ain't they?"

Mike walked outside and stopped at the first payphone that wasn't occupied. He dropped four quarters into it, and dialed Stutter Bug's home phone number. He lived down in Columbia, AKA the Metro.

Mike had met Stutter Bug back at the Greenville Group Home when they were both teens. Stutter Bug's whole family was turned out on everything from crack to heroin, so he had been in the streets since he was small, just like Mike. They had automatically clicked when they met, despite Bug's speech impediment. The two of them would often buy weed and then smoke out in their room together, blowing each other shotguns from the blunts.

After doing about six months at the group home, Bug was sent back to Columbia to live with a relative who said they'd take him in. But before he left, he gave Mike his people's number and told him that if he was ever in the Met to get in touch with him, so he could show him how live his city was.

A few years later, Mike decided to see what Bug was up to, and called him. Stutter Bug was staying in a notorious housing project called Saxon Homes. Mike went through and chilled down there in the Metro for a few days. He spent his time there getting high, going to clubs like Columbia Live and The Palace, and fucking them

Metro bitches.

On the day Mike was getting ready to leave, Stutter Bug called him into the kitchen of his apartment in Saxon Homes, and showed him a crate full of machine guns, bullets, pistols, and all other types of weaponry. He told Mike this was his new hustle, and that if he ever needed some guns to holla at him, and he'd make sure he got a good deal. So anytime Mike needed some good shit that wasn't hot, he got with Bug and they did business.

The phone rang five times before it was answered. "Hello?"

"Bug, it's me nigga, Mike. What's happenin'?!"

"Oh sh-shit! What's up my n-n-n-n-nigga? What's g-g-good?"

"Hey Bug, look here, man. Some shit just went down up here, and I need to know if I can come through and get some of that shit I got from you last time," said Mike, purposefully avoiding saying anything that might be used against him in a court of law.

"Yeah, y-y-y-you know what it is, my n-nigga. Whatever you need, I got you. Matter fact I j-j-just got some new shit in."

"Say no mo' then. I'll be through later on today, ya' heard?"

"Th-that's what it is then."

Mike hung up the phone, and went back into the hospital to let Ant D know what the business was.

Chapter 20

Columbia, better known as "The Metro", was the state of South Carolina's capitol. The city had a population of about 450,000 people, and it was located dead in the center of the state. Doing the speed limit, it was about an hour and a half drive from Greenville.

That afternoon at around 5:30, Mike and Ant D got off on the exit that put them on Broad River Road. That took them directly into the heart of the city. They had rented a U-haul truck for the trip because they didn't want to attract any extra attention from the police by driving their own cars. The pigs in Columbia were just as racist as the redneck cops back home in the Ville.

Ant D pulled the truck into a gas station so Mike could call Stutter Bug and let him know that they were in town. They had to find out where to meet him.

After he made the call, Mike came back to the truck, got in, and told Ant how to get to a hotel in West Columbia called Knights Inn. Twenty minutes later, Ant pulled into the Knights Inn parking lot and stopped in front of room number 34. They both got out, and Mike went over and knocked on the door.

Mike saw somebody peep from behind the curtains before the door opened. It was Stutter Bug. He stood about 5'8", was dark skinned, and had a low cut ceaser with waves. He was a little heavy for his size, but he was always quick to point out that it never stopped him from getting no pussy, so he wasn't too concerned about it.

Mike walked into the room first. Ant D walked in behind him, and closed the door. "M-m-m-mike, what's happenin', my n-n-n-n-nigga?" asked Bug as he gave Mike a pound and hug. "D-d-d-damn it's been a m-m-m-minute since I seen yo' ass, n-n-n-nigga! What's good?"

"Ain't shit good right now, Bug. Yo, this is my folk right here, Ant D. This nigga like a fuckin' brother to me, ya heard?"

"W-w-w-what's up, dog," said Bug.

"Ain't shit," replied Ant D tersely. He was ready to handle business, get what they had come for, and get the fuck back home. His sister was lying up in a hospital bed damn near dead, and he was ready to make somebody bleed. The small talk and chit chatter could wait for another time.

Picking up on his homey's demeanor, Mike said, "So what you got for us, Bug? Let's go 'head and handle this business."

Stutter Bug walked them over to the bed, where he had a large assortment of guns and ammunition laid out on display. There were a couple of AK-47's, two AR-15's, three black Glock 9mm's, four nickel plated 45's, an Uzi, and a sawed off double barrel shotgun. And that's not even getting into all of the ammo. There were 30, 40, and 75 round drum magazines available for each assault rifle. Bug also had cases of shotgun shells, shell catchers, and some night vision goggles. He had detachable pistol grips, and threaded barrels for the attachment of a flash suppressor for the AR. That crazy ass nigga even had grenades sitting on the bed!

"Goddamn Bug, where the fuck you think we goin', to muh 'fuckin Afghanistan, or some shit?!" joked Mike.

"N-n-n-n-n-never know what you might need," said Bug. He smiled and revealed a chipped tooth.

"You ain't got no vests?" asked Ant D

Bug walked over to the bathroom, and came back with two Kevlar bulletproof vests. Ant and Mike talked amongst each other for a minute, and then finally decided on the two AR's, two Glocks, which were Mike's favorite gun, the sawed off, the Uzi, and both vests. Then they racked up on ammunition. They were like two tricks in a house full of pussy!

"W-w-w-w-what y'all wanna do 'bout the grenades though? Y-y'all straight on them?"

Ant and Mike looked at each other, and then smiled. "Fuck it, let's get em!" they said in unison.

Bug packed everything into a large wooden crate with cellophane packaging, while Mike peeled the money for the merchandise from a stack of bills. After paying Bug the agreed upon price, plus a little extra for coming through on such short notice, Mike and Ant D took the crate outside, put it into the back of the truck, and then hopped in the front.

Before they pulled off, Bug hollered at Mike and told him that once they took care of their business, to come back to the Met and chill for a minute. "M-m-m-me and my folk just opened a night club called Th-th-the G-Spot. Nothin' but the best f-food, the best drink, and the best p-p-p-pussy, ya' heard?"

"That's what it is, Bug. As soon as this shit right here get handled, we probably gonna need to get away for a lil' minute anyway. So we'll be back through," said Mike, giving Bug a pound. Ant D started the U-Haul up, and pulled out of the parking lot onto the main road. They headed for the interstate that would take them back to the UPS.

$$$

At 11:30 P.M. Ant D pulled into his mama's driveway back in the District, relieved at having made it back home without being stopped by the police. There was no telling how much time they would have got if they were caught with the type of shit they were riding around with. Those dumb ass crackers might've even thought they were fucking terrorists recruited by Bin Laden or the fucking Taliban.

All of the lights were out, and the house looked completely deserted. And since Glo refused to leave the hospital until Meka woke up out of her coma, it was. She had been there earlier, to pick up a change of clothes and some hygiene products, and then she headed right back to the hospital to be by her daughter's side. She hadn't been there for her daughter when she was growing up, but she was damn sure going to be there for her now.

Mike and Ant D got out and headed towards the rear of the truck to get the crate out so they could take it inside. As they were pulling it out, a candy apple red convertible Benz pulled up to the curb. It was Sylvia Brown, the owner of Sylvia's Hair and Nail Salon. She waved and said, "Hey y'all, what's going on?"

"Ain't nothin', Sylvia. Same shit, different toilet, ya' dig? Just tryna flush this muh'fucka, ya' know?"

"Yeah, I hear that. Somebody moving or somethin'?" asked Sylvia, being nosey as usual.

"Naw, ain't nobody moving, Sylvia. Why you ask that?"

"Because when I pulled up I saw y'all pullin' a big ass crate outta that U-Haul truck. So I figured somebody was moving."

"Sylvia, let me ask you a question real quick," said Ant D. "Why the fuck is you so nosey? You done stopped doin' hair, and started workin' for the Sheriff's office, or some shit?"

"Damn Ant, calm yo' ass down! I was just asking, damn! Anyways, tell Meka she need to come get her truck out my parking lot for somebody steal it. That lil' pink Range Rover been sittin' there since Saturday, and I ain't gonna be responsible if anything happens to it. Y'all know how trifling muh'fuckas is. They'll have that shit stripped, and sitting on bricks befo' long. Where Meka at anyway?"

Mike and Ant looked at each other. As meddlesome as Sylvia was, it was highly unlikely that she hadn't already heard about what had happened to Meka. So more than likely, she was just playing dumb in order to see what additional information she could get.

After a few seconds, it hit Ant that this would be the perfect opportunity to put his plan in motion. And what better person to get the word out than Sylvia, with her big ass mouth? Ant said, "Mike, go 'head and tell her what's poppin', dog. I'm finna run in the house and grab somethin' real quick." Ant D took off for the house, leaving Mike to explain the situation to Sylvia.

"So what's going on, Mike," asked Sylvia, salivating with anticipation at the juicy gossip she was about to receive. "Is Meka okay?" Sylvia lit up a Newport 100 and took a deep pull. She exhaled the smoke into the air, waiting for Mike to talk. He told her as much as he felt she needed to know to put the word out in the street, but without going into a whole bunch of details. Some shit was just better left unsaid, especially when dealing with somebody with a mouth like Sylvia's.

Five minutes later, Ant D came out of the house with a plastic Bi-Lo shopping bag filled with money. "Mike told you what time it is, right?"

"Yeah, but who'd do something like that to Meka? And why?"

"That's what we tryna find out," said Ant. He opened the plastic bag, and revealed the money to a wide eyed Sylvia. "You see that? That's a hun'ned stacks right there on deck, cash money. We tryna find out who them pussy niggas was that did that shit to my sister. Whoever comes through with some reliable information we can use, the money's theirs, ya' heard?"

"We want you to put the word out for us, Sylvia," Mike said.

"Oh, y'all know I'ma do that. This the best gossip I done got all year. Shiiiiiiit, with that much money, if I hear something I'll tell you myself. I could use that money for real. Especially with the holidays coming up."

"That's what it is then. Get at us if you hear somethin', Sylvia."

"Oh most definitely," she replied. "Oh yeah! Before I forget, y'all know tomorrow Shawn's funeral, right?"

"Naw, we ain't even know that shit," said Mike. "But that was our nigga, so you know we gon' come through and show some love."

"Fa' sho', man. Shawn wasn't even supposed to have died like that," said Ant. "That nigga could'a had made it to the N.B.A or some shit, fa' real. But you know what's really crazy? After a while, you lose so many niggas that you kinda' become numb to that shit. Shit don't even mean nothin' no mo'…"

There was a moment of silence as the gravity of Ant D's statement sunk in. He and Mike reflected on all the niggas they'd known that had fell victim to the streets in one way or another. Either dead, strung out, or in jail with a number so big that they might as well have been in the grave. This was the unfortunate reality of life when you lived and survived in an impoverished neighborhood, where the cycle of death, either mental or physical, seemed to never end. But they were given this world, they didn't make it.

After her own brief moment of reflection, Sylvia inhaled on her Newport. As she exhaled, she broke the silence by saying, "Well, I guess I'll see y'all at the funeral then."

She slowly pulled away from the curb. Before she had even reached the end of the street, she had her cell phone out, running her mouth. "Girlllll, wait 'til I tell you what done happened now!"

After getting the crate inside the house, Mike and Ant D inspected and cleaned their newly purchased arsenal before putting everything back into the box, and placing it inside Ant's closet.

Looking at the diamond encrusted bezel on his watch. Mike saw that it was past midnight. He suddenly remembered that he was supposed to have made a call earlier. Ant D was in the kitchen emptying a whole box of Lucky Charms into a large bowl that Gloria used to mix cake batter in. He got the milk from the fridge, poured it into the bowl, got him a spoon, and then took his dinner into the living room to bust that shit down. He put his favorite movie, "Scarface", into the DVD player, and took a snort of coke off a twenty dollar bill before he began watching it for the thousandth time.

Mike was beginning to notice that Ant was fucking with that "white girl" a lot more often now. And Mike knew how easy it was for that "girl" to turn into a bitch that wouldn't leave, no matter how hard you tried to throw her out. He wasn't going to let his best friend turn into no coke head. He couldn't let him go out like that.

He'd have to talk to that nigga about that shit soon.

Mike pulled out his cell phone and dialed the number Nikki had given him the day before at the park. Meanwhile, Ant noisily continued eating his cereal beside him on the couch watching Al Pacino brilliantly play a refugee Cuban on the come up.

On the seventh ring Mike heard Nikki's tired voice answer the phone. "Hello?"

"Hey, Nikki, it's me," said Mike.

"Me who?"

"It's Mike, Nikki. Damn, you done forgot my voice that fast?"

"Oh no, I didn't forget your voice Mike. It's just that I was expecting you to call me a lot earlier than this. It's late, and I was sleeping. I'm not used to getting calls this late in the night," said Nikki with an attitude, irritated that Mike had waited so late to call. Any call past 10 O'clock from a dude was a booty call to Nikki. And after the conversation they'd had the other night, she really hoped that Mike wasn't trying no shit like that.

"Yeah, that's my bad, Nikki. I had meant to call you earlier, but there's been a lot of shit going on today that I had to deal with."

Thinking that this was just some lame ass excuse, she said, "Yeah? Like what?"

Briefly Mike went into what had happened to Meka, and the time he'd spent at the hospital with Glo and Ant D. Hearing the raw emotion in Mike's voice, the irritation in Nikki's own voice quickly melted away into concern. "Oh my God! Is she going to be alright?"

"We don't even know yet. We gotta wait and find out."

"Mike, I'm really sorry I came off on you like that a second ago. I had no idea what you've been going through."

"You ain't gotta apologize. I still should'a called you earlier."

"So how are you feeling? Are you ok?"

"I'm dealing wit' it," Mike said, as images of Meka's swollen body lying up in that hospital bed flashed through his mind.

After a few seconds of silence, Nikki said, "Mike, do you want to come over and talk about it?"

"I thought you stayed wit' your mama and lil' brother."

"I do, but they're both out of town visiting with some of my family in Florida. So I'm here by myself for the next few days."

"Ok, I'll come over. But you gotta make me a promise."

"What?"

"You gotta promise me that if I come over, that you won't try to take advantage of me," joked Mike.

Nikki laughed, and said, "Ok, I promise." But she had her fingers crossed.

Chapter 21

After he got Ant to drop him off at the hospital so he could retrieve his Escalade from the parking lot he left it in earlier that day, Mike rode out to Nikki's apartment complex in Berea. Once he got there, he killed the ignition, got out and walked over to apartment # 37.

Just as he was getting ready to knock on the door, Nikki opened it and greeted him with a hug. She was wearing a white baby doll tee-shirt and a pair of tight pink panties. It wasn't expensive lingerie, but it didn't need to be. Nikki was one of those rare girls who looked sexy no matter what she had on. She was a modern-day Stacey Dash. Pretty face, green eyes, dimpled smile, and a tight, beautiful body. She gleefully said, "Hey Mike."

Mike returned the affection and immediately became aroused by feeling Nikki's warm, soft body pressed against his.

She noticed Mike's developing erection, and said, "Let's go inside." She pulled Mike towards the living room, so he kicked the door closed behind him and locked it.

A few steps into the living room, Mike gently grabbed Nikki by the waist and turned her around so that she was facing him. Nikki stood up on her tip toes, leaned in and slipped her tongue inside Mike's mouth, and gave him a slow, sensuous kiss.

While they passionately explored each other's mouths, Mike let his hand drop from Nikki's waist to her soft round ass, gently squeezing and rubbing each cheek through the soft fabric of her underwear. Nikki felt a fire slowly begin to burn between her legs, and within a matter of seconds the front of her panties were noticeably wet with the moisture of her arousal. Slowly she pulled away from Mike.

"What's up, Nikki? What's wrong?" He didn't want to let her out of his arms. He was loving the way she felt next to him.

"Nothing's wrong, Mike. It's just that, if this is going to be our first time, I want it to be special."

"This *is* special. Me and you together, and we both feelin' the same thing at the same time. What's mo' special than that?" He pulled her back towards him. Mike bent his head down and kissed Nikki's forehead, and then worked his way down her face. He kissed her closed eyelids, her nose, her lips, and then began to suck softly on her neck.

Nikki's eyes remained closed, and she gasped at the pleasure that Mike was giving her body. After a moment it became too intense for her to bear. She jumped up in Mike's arms, and wrapped her legs around his waist. She whispered in his ear, "Take me upstairs."

Mike carried Nikki up the stairs to her bedroom, and gently laid her down on her queen-sized bed. He began taking off his clothes, so Nikki smiled at him and did the same. When she came out of her T-shirt, her full, ripe C-cup breasts with dime sized nipples were revealed, proving she was braless.

Mike looked at Nikki lying there on the bed, and couldn't believe how incredibly sexy she was. It was like she had no flaws. He hurriedly pulled his boxers off and got onto the bed with Nikki, lying between her legs. Using his forearms to support his weight, Mike leaned down and slipped his tongue in her mouth again, savoring her taste.

Feeling his erection rubbing up against her stomach, Nikki lifted her hips and pulled her moist panties off. Mike immediately tried to get inside of her. In his haste, he missed the entry altogether. Nikki reached down between their naked bodies and grabbed Mike's throbbing dick. She guided him inside of her already well lubricated pussy. Mike couldn't believe how tight she was, or how good she felt. He began to quickly thrust in and out of her.

Nikki whispered into his ear, "Slow down, baby, you don't have to rush. Take your time. I'm not going anywhere."

Mike slowed down the tempo and started making passionate love to Nikki. She wrapped her legs around his waist, using her pelvis to match the grinding of his slow steady thrusts inside of her. She looked Mike in his face and bit her bottom lip in ecstasy. Every time he went deep inside of Nikki's wetness he rubbed against her clit, causing her to lose her mind with pleasure. The feeling was so good that she didn't want it to stop. But her tightness already had Mike on the brink of a powerful ejaculation. He tried to hold it back, but it was no use. In seconds, he was cumming violently inside of her. Nikki was far from disappointed though. She saw this as an opportunity to give back the pleasure she'd received, and at the same time get him ready for round two.

When Mike rolled over onto his back, Nikki got up on her knees and began kissing all over his body. She licked and sucked on his nipples, and kissed her way down her lover's torso. When she got to his dick, which was limp and wet with her juices, she kissed that too, before putting it into her mouth. Nikki was far from experienced when it came to giving head, and it showed. But just the fact that she was willing to please him like that was enough to revive Mike's erection.

Once she saw that he was ready for another round, Nikki mounted him so that she was on top facing him. Slowly she rode his rejuvenated dick up and down, and back and forth, loving the way he filled her up and stretched her insides. Nikki looked into Mike's eyes and sped up the pace, going faster and faster until she reached her first orgasm of the night - but not her last...

For the rest of the night, and into the early morning, Nikki and Mike explored each other's body. They each learned what turned the other on until finally, out of sheer exhaustion, they fell asleep in each other's arms.

Chapter 22

The sky was overcast with sadness as tears drizzled down from the heavens and fell upon the earth, wetting the many mourners who had gathered to see Shawn Christopher McGee's body laid to rest. Closest to the rich mahogany wooden casket, standing under umbrellas in the front row was Shawn's family. He never knew his dad but his mama, Renee, his two younger sisters, Ashley and Angela, and his grandparents, Ruth and Gerald McGee, were there. Renee was crying uncontrollably, her salty tears mixing with the rain as they trickled down her weary face. Her daughters had to hold her up in order to keep her from falling to the ground. She was overwhelmed with the indescribable feeling of grief. Seeing her only son getting ready to be placed into the ground from which he came was unbearable.

Standing on the grass behind the family were over a hundred mourners whom Shawn had touched in some way or another throughout his short life. Coaches, school faculty, old girlfriends, and numerous homeboys wearing black R.I.P. tee-shirts with Shawn's photo on the front of them were all in attendance. Some of the people there hadn't even met Shawn personally, but had seen him on the local news, or read about him in The Greenville Newspaper so much that they felt as if they had. They had lived vicariously through him and his many exploits on the basketball court, and now it was suddenly over. Cut short by a bullet that didn't even have his name on it.

Among the many mourners who had gathered at the cemetery were Ant D and Mike, who had known Shawn for years. Shawn had always been cool with them, but he had never been in the streets like them. He might've gone to a party every now and then and had a few beers, but overall he was a good dude that went to school, got the grades, got the girls, and was on his way out the 'hood to a better life. He wasn't supposed to be laid up in that casket like that... but he was. Shit like that tended to happen in the 'hood so often that it made Ant D wonder if there really was a God.

"...And so we gather here today... not to mourn the life of a young man that is no longer here with us physically, but to *celebrate* the life of a young man whose memories will be here with us long after his body has returned to the dirt from which God Almighty has created us all. Let us not cry any tears for young Shawn. Instead, let us smile and rejoice at the fact that his soul is now with the Heavenly Father in paradise...at peace," said the dark skinned, heavyset preacher affectionately called Pastor Johnson.

He continued. "And let this be a wakeup call to all of us, especially to our youth, that life is a precious gift given to us by the Lord, that shouldn't be taken for granted. It's a gift that should be appreciated and cherished. For we never know when it will be our time to meet the Heavenly Father..."

Pastor Johnson took a brief reprise from his sermon to take a long look into the crowd. It seemed as if he was looking into each individual's soul, and searching. "I'm tired, y'all... I said I'm tired, y'all! Tired of the killing, and tired of the senseless violence in our communities! How many more young Black men and women am I going to have to bury?! And for what?! For what?! We're killing one another for nothing! It's a cycle that's been going on since the days of slavery, but we can no longer blame the White man. We're doing it to ourselves! Brothers and sisters, this madness must stop! Oh, Lord knows I'm tired of seeing mothers burying their sons and daughters, before they even get the chance to find out what life is all about."

Shawn's mother was crying hysterically now, her family doing their best to console her and keep her from falling to the ground.

"So before we leave this afternoon, I would like to lead everybody in a much needed prayer. Every head bowed, every eye closed… Lord God, we come to you today as sinners, as murderers, as robbers, as drug dealers, and adulterers. But we know all of that means nothing to you. You died so that our sins might be wiped clean. We come to you today, O Lord, to ask for forgiveness, and to ask for understanding in these trying times. To ask for guidance as we travel down this tumultuous road called life. Lord, please help us see things as you would have us see them, and not with our own misguided sight. Thy kingdom come, Thy will be done. On Earth as it is in Heaven…Amen."

The mourners opened their eyes. More than a few had tears in them, deeply affected by Pastor Johnson's words. For a moment there was a long silence, as everyone in attendance reflected back on the words that had just been spoken so eloquently and heartfelt by the pastor.

His words were like seeds being planted in the fertile soil of some of the youth in attendance. Of course some of the ground had been too hardened by the circumstances of their lives to take root, but a few seeds had managed to penetrate a few cold, embittered hearts.

An up and coming R&B group from the 'Ville called Black Soul broke out into a heartfelt rendition of an old hit called "Gangsta Lean", as the mourners filed pass the casket to take one last look at the life that had been taken from them too soon. Despite the song's secular title, it sounded like pure gospel coming from the four young men's mouths'. Their harmony was beautiful.

"*This song's dedicated… to my homey in that gangsta lean. Why'd you have to go so sooooooooon? It seemed like yesterday we were hangin' round the hoooooood – Now I'm gonna keep your memory alive like a homey shoooooooould… This is for my homey… See you when I get there…*"

Mike stared at Shawn's serene face as he walked past his opened casket, and wondered why it wasn't him lying in that box. For once in his life, he seriously contemplated his own mortality and wondered where the hell he was going. He wondered what kind of plan God had in store for *him*.

$$$

Over the next weeks, Ant D and Mike waited to hear some news concerning who had left Meka in that trash can for dead. Mike also spent a lot of time with Nikki. He enjoyed her company more than any other girl he'd ever been with. The way she smelled, the way she walked, the way she talked, her smile… Everything about her had him intrigued. Against his better judgment, he was falling in love.

After a while, it became impossible for them to have any privacy at her mama's house, so Mike asked Nikki to move in with him. She said yes, and of course after that their bond became even stronger. Nikki would wake up in the morning, cook them breakfast, and then be off to class at Greenville Tech. When she got home, they would often take hot bubble baths or showers together. When Mike would sit down on the couch to watch TV, Nikki would lie on the couch too and put her feet up in his lap. Mike would massage her soft pedicured feet while the two of them laughed at re-runs of "Martin" and "In Living Color."

Over time, their relationship continued to grow. It got to the point where Mike found himself telling Nikki about his life and dreams as they lay in the bed listening to her favorite album, *The Diary of Alicia Keys.*

"I won't tell your secrets. Your secrets are safe with me-e. I won't tell your secrets - just think of me as the pages in your diary…"

It was more than just the bomb sex they shared. It was the fact that they actually clicked, both mentally and emotionally. Mike had never experienced anything like that before. He was surprised at how willing he was to remain faithful to Nikki.

Nowadays the word "love" is completely overused, but that's what their thing was becoming… Anybody's who's ever been in a real relationship, and really genuinely cared and loved that other person, could relate to what Mike and Nikki were experiencing.

On the date of October 26th, Nikki came out of the bathroom and told Mike that she was pregnant, not exactly sure how he would take the news. Mike was overjoyed that she informed him that he was finally going to get a chance to be what nobody ever was to him… a father. Together, he and Nikki celebrated. But unfortunately, the celebration wouldn't last long.

Chapter 23

That same morning at 9:32 A.M. Gloria was sitting in a cushioned chair next to Meka's bed reading the latest hot urban novel from Synergy Publications, when she thought she heard somebody say something. She figured she had to be hearing things because there was nobody else in the room besides her and Meka. So she went back to reading her book.

"Mama..." Gloria jumped, startled by the sound of her daughter's voice, which she hadn't heard in a very long time. That time she knew she wasn't imagining things. She dropped her paperback on the floor, and turned to look at Meka, who's eyes were wide open and staring at her.

"Mama..."

Meka had been admitted into the hospital back on September 3rd. Since then, the severe swelling had gone down, and the bruises and cuts had healed. The only real signs of what had happened to her were her four missing top teeth, and a scar on her forehead. Other than that, she appeared to be the same Meka. At least physically. Psychologically, no one knew how long it would take her mind to heal, or if it ever would. All of the doctors had said that she'd need reconstructive surgery, but they were obviously wrong. She had healed well over the last weeks.

Glo thanked God silently, and then she grabbed Meka's hand, and said, "Hey baby, how you feelin'?"

"Like I just got hit by an 18 wheeler," she replied hoarsely. It was going to take Meka a minute to get her voice back right, after not using her vocal chords for so long.

"Let me go get the doctor and tell him you up, baby. I'll be right back." Glo was overjoyed.

When she left out of the room, Meka wiggled her toes and fingers to make sure she still had them all, and that they still worked. She closed her eyes for a second, and images of what Rico and them had done to her played vividly in her mind. The scene was so clear that it was like she was reliving it all over again. Not a single tear escaped her eyes though. Naw, fuck that. The time for crying was over. And the time for revenge had just begun.

Gloria walked back into the room with two nurses and Dr. Baker, who had been Meka's doctor since she was first admitted. "Well, well, well. Sleeping Beauty is awake," said Dr. Baker, smiling. "How are you feeling, Tameka?"

"I'm real sore, and my voice is really hoarse, but other than that I'm good."

"Well, the soreness is to be expected from you being immobilized for so long. The same thing goes for your voice. Your vocal chords are muscles, and any muscle that is not used on a regular basis atrophies."

"Uhhh, doc, could you say that in English, please."

"Well, Tameka, it's like this. With a little rehabilitation and exercise, you'll be as good as new in no time." Dr. Baker was elated at seeing one of his patients pull through. That didn't happen often in a case like Meka's.

Dr. Baker checked Meka's vitals and her reflexes, and then briefly looked into her pupils with a small penlight. Seeing that everything appeared normal, the doctor left, along with the two nurses, who said they'd be back later to start her rehabilitation.

As soon as they were out of the room, Meka asked her mother where Ant D and Mike were at. "Well, your brother is probably at the house. Him and Mike ain't really been doing too much since this happened. They've been waiting for you to pull through," said Glo. "Mike done started messin' with some girl named Nikki, but other than that it's been the same ole' same ole'."

"Mama, call Ant and tell him I'm up, and that we need to talk. Tell him to make sure Mike comes with him too," said Meka, with nothing but revenge on her mind...

$$$

As soon as Ant D got off the phone with his mama, he dialed Mike's number.

"Hello?" answered Nikki.

"Hey Nikki, it's me. Let me holla' at Mike real quick."

Hearing the intensity in Ant's voice, Nikki knew something was up. Besides that, Ant D never got out of bed that early. Never.

"Ant, what's going on?" asked Nikki.

"Ain't shit. I just need to holla' at Mike 'bout somethin' real quick, ya' heard?"

"Umm hmm," said Nikki skeptically. "Hold on for a second, he's in the shower," she said walking to the bathroom.

Ant was happy that his homey had found somebody he'd ride for and all that, but all of that Brian McKnight, Ne-Yo, R&B shit wasn't for him. "Skeet it then beat it" was Ant D's motto, and he hadn't met a bitch yet to make him change that. Besides, Ant D considered being in love a weakness that he couldn't afford to indulge himself in.

"Only wife of mine is a life of crime," Ant mumbled to himself, quoting a line from one of his favorite rappers, Jay-Z.

Mike's voice came on the line. "What's up, homey?"

"Meka's outta her coma. She told my mama that she had to see us, and that she had somethin' to tell us. You already know what it is, my nigga. Time to get this shit poppin', ya' heard? You *is* still ready to ride, ain't you?" questioned Ant, hoping that a little in-house pussy hadn't turned his best man soft.

"Come on, nigga, you ain't even gotta ask me no shit like that. Meka *my* sister too. I'ma ride 'til the wheels fall off. Ain't shit changed."

"Say no mo'. I'll see you at the hospital then," said Ant, and pressed the end button on his phone. He leaned over the side of the bed and used a rolled up hundred dollar bill to snort a line of coke off a tray on the nightstand.

Mike handed the cordless phone back to Nikki, and stepped out of the shower. He wrapped a towel around his waist, and then proceeded into the bedroom, where he began to get dressed.

Nikki stood in the doorway with her hand on her hip watching Mike as he silently put his clothes on. The happiness and excitement that they'd shared earlier, after finding out that she was pregnant, had evaporated with Ant's call. "Mike, what's going on, baby? What did Ant want?"

"Meka just came outta her coma. I'm finna meet him at the hospital."

"That's good news, but you don't seem too excited, so what's really going on?" she asked.

"Listen baby, I told you from day one that I'd never lie to you. And I ain't fixin' to start now. Now that Meka's outta her coma, we gonna find out who did that shit to her. And whoever it was is gonna pay. It's that simple."

"Pay how? Mike, *please* tell me that you're not thinking about doing anything crazy."

"Nikki, come here." She walked over to the foot of the bed where Mike was sitting, and sat on his lap. Mike said, "Baby, look. In these streets, if niggas hurt somebody that you care about, you gotta get at 'em. It's that simple. Meka like the sister I never had. Ain't no way I'm finna let that shit go down like that."

"Why not let the police deal with it?" asked Nikki naively, not understanding the unwritten rules of the street. She wrapped her arms around Mike's neck.

"See that's the thing, Nikki. Once you start livin' this life right here, there's codes you gotta live by. You don't go to the police fa' shit. *Nothing*, I don't care what the situation is. Besides, the police don't give a fuck about us no way. That's what these clown ass niggas that be snitchin' fail to realize. Niggas be actin' like they fuckin' killas and gorillas, but when shit gets hot, they asses turn into fuckin' chumps and chimps. They start singing to the pigs like they tryna start a new R&B group or something. They got the rules to the game fucked up. But as long as I'm out here in these streets, I'ma stay true to 'em."

"Stay true to what, Mike? To what?! These streets don't give a fuck about you!! *I* do! What about me?! What about the baby? What about staying true to us," pleaded Nikki, looking deep into Mike's eyes.

Frustrated that Nikki couldn't understand the values that had governed his life for so long, Mike got up and told her they'd talk about it later.

She argued, "What if there is no later, Mike? You don't have to go. Stay here with me, baby. *Please.*" He wrapped his arms around Nikki and held her close, in her embrace finding reprieve from a life of abandonment and pain from not being wanted, and not being loved. He wished he could make her understand how important it was to retaliate for Meka, but she was from a totally different world. They held each other in silence, neither wanting to let the other go.

All of a sudden…*BOOM!* The front door of the apartment imploded, and police in blue uniforms and black vests with yellow writing on them that read Greenville County swarmed into the apartment with their guns drawn. Mike's first instinct was to go for his gun, but Nikki was there with him. He didn't want to jeopardize her life, or the life of his unborn child. For he had no doubt that those scary ass, trigger happy, crooked ass cops wouldn't hesitate to kill them both, and have their deaths ruled "justifiable homicide." He'd seen it happen too many times. So when they pointed their guns at him and Nikki and yelled "*Sheriff's Office, get on the ground—NOW!!*", he followed their instructions and got on the ground. Crying uncontrollably and confused, Nikki did the same. The officers forcefully pulled their arms behind their backs, and using more force than necessary, placed cuffs on them both.

"Mike, what's going on?"

"Nikki, everything…"

"Shut the fuck up, boy," yelled one of the officers, as he grabbed Mike by the arm and snatched him up on his feet. His pink face only inches from Mike's, he said, "Your ass is goin' down, mother-fucker! We got your fuckin' ass now, boy! I bet next time your ass will stop when you're supposed to!" The officer's breath stank, and spittle flew from his mouth into Mike's face as he spoke.

Mike looked directly into the cop's eyes, and returned his hateful glare. He said, "As soon as I make bail, I'ma make sure to stop by your mama's house and get some of that good head she got. Heard that bitch can suck a mean dick. It's too bad she ain't do the world a favor and swallow yo' sorry cracker ass…"

Before he could say another word, the cop sucker punched Mike in the gut, causing him to double over in pain.

"Get their sorry asses out of here! And don't forget to read 'em their goddamn rights! I don't want no fuckin' technicalities biting us in the ass later on."

Chapter 24

The ride downtown to the county jail was one that Mike had taken on numerous occasions over the years as a juvenile offender, so it really wasn't a big deal to him. Taking chances, and living the life that he and so many others like him lived on a daily basis, it was an inevitability that sooner or later you would get locked up. Almost every black male in the 'hood at some point in time had to experience the inhumanity of being caged like a wild animal. Somehow over the years, doing a bid had become a badge of honor, provided you went in and came back like a man. It was a rite of passage into manhood. That misguided way of thinking was what had so many young brothers doing 35, 50, and 75 years without parole; never to see the outside streets again.

Though Mike could more than handle himself, it was Nikki that he was mostly concerned about, as they approached the jail in separate cars. She was the type of girl that had never been in any type of trouble in her entire life, so he could only imagine what was going through her mind right now. Whatever it took, he had to see to it that she didn't get mixed up in any of the charges they were getting ready to throw at him. The thought alone of her riding in the back of that police car, with his unborn child in her womb, behind some bullshit he did pained him more than any physical pain he'd ever experienced.

Once at the county jail, both Mike and Nikki were placed into separate holding cells. The holding cells were tiny concrete boxes that reeked of sweat, vomit, and urine. They were rarely, if ever, cleaned. The walls were filthy and littered with years of graffiti, dirt, and only God knew what else. That was where the "suspects" were kept until they faced arraignment, a process in which they were taken before a judge, told of the charges that were being brought against them, and whether or not they would be eligible for bond.

Mike didn't know exactly what the charges against him were, but whatever they were, he knew he'd have to take responsibility in order for them to let Nikki go.

After hours upon hours of waiting in that nasty ass holding cell to be called (a subtle tactic often used by the police to coerce confessions and information out of individuals), finally Mike was pulled out, handcuffed, and walked down the hallway by a deputy to the judge's chamber.

"Ok, let's see what we have here," said Judge Anderson. He looked down at the stack of warrants in front of him, as he sat behind the elevated judge's bench. "Failure to stop for a blue light, reckless endangerment while driving, unlawful possession of a firearm, possession of marijuana…" The litany of charges being read by the bespectacled, balding, Judge Anderson went on and on. Mike just looked up at him with a blank stare. Unfortunately this was a position Mike was all too familiar with, so he knew the protocol: remain silent.

After all the indictments were read, Judge Anderson looked down at Mike and asked, "Do you understand all the charges that I just read, that are being brought against you?"

Mike remained silent.

"Now, I understand that there was also a young lady at the scene of the arrest… So Mr. Smith, I'm going to do you a favor. You have two choices. You can either own up to the drugs and guns in your apartment that were found… or she can take the fall with you, and y'all can spend the next twenty years being pen pals in the Department of Corrections. The choice is yours."

Without even a moment of thought or hesitation, Mike looked directly into the eyes of the old pale faced judge, and finally broke his silence. "Everything in the apartment was mine."

"Are you absolutely sure about what you're saying, Mr. Smith? You have been advised of your rights, and stated that you understood them. As you know, anything you say can and will be used against you in any future proceedings."

Mike knew that admitting to the fact that everything the officers found upon their search of his apartment was his was an open admission of guilt that could not be taken back later, but he also knew it would free Nikki, so he never even thought twice. "Yeah, I'm sure. And I understand my rights and all that, so can we just go 'head and skip all this Law & Order bullshit, and get this over wit', man?"

There was a brief moment of silence as the judge busied himself signing off on some papers. Finally he said, "Bail set at $150,000!" and banged his gavel down. "Deputy, would you please get this worthless piece of shit out of my sight."

"Gladly, your honor." The guard grabbed Mike roughly by the arm, and led him out of the judge's chamber.

They headed down a corridor, and then were buzzed through two heavily fortified double doors. Mike was led into the reception area where the dehumanizing process known as "intake" would begin. He got ready to have his mug shot taken, be fingerprinted, and strip searched.

$$$

Almost a full day had passed since Nikki was arrested with Mike. She hadn't seen him since they had both been placed into separate squad cars, and taken to the county jail. Her worse fears had become a reality. She'd been crying so much in that tiny, soiled cell that her eyes were red and puffy. She had no more tears left to cry, so she pulled her knees up to her chest and rocked back and forth in the corner. Nikki was exhausted, both mentally and physically.

She hadn't even bothered touching the disgusting jail house trays of food they had been periodically pushing through a small opening at the bottom of the door.

"Jones…Nikki Jones…" It sounded as if someone was calling her name from some far, far away place. It was a female's voice, but Nikki wasn't sure where the sound was coming from so she kept her head buried between her knees and prayed that her horrible ordeal would be over soon.

"Miss Jones," said the voice, "you're being released." As the words the guard had just spoken gradually registered in her brain, Nikki looked up and finally noticed the female guard who was standing at the entrance. She was so out of it that she hadn't even heard the heavy metal door when it was opened, let alone noticed the guard standing there. "Did you hear what I said, Ms. Jones? You're being released."

"Released?" Nikki knew what the word meant but after hours upon hours of solitary confinement, it seemed foreign somehow. Slowly, she got to her feet. She felt as if she was emerging from a dream, or a nightmare rather. Nikki followed the guard out of the cell.

$$$

"Nigga, is you listenin' to what I'm sayin'?! The po-lice kicked in my door, and arrested me and Nikki," said Mike to Ant D, while using the phone at the guard's desk where they did the processing. That was one of the few advantages of being locked up in Greenville County. More than likely one of the guards, who were predominately young and Black, had gone to school with you, had heard of you, or knew somebody that was related to you. So after Mike was dressed out in an orange jumpsuit and matching flip flops, he approached the desk and saw his homegirl Brandy Harris from Brutontown sitting there waiting to process him.

Mike had quickly and discreetly, as there were eyes and ears everywhere in the detention center - both real and electronic, explained his situation. He told her that he'd throw her a little paper when he got out if she would let him use the staff phone to make a call instead of the inmate phone, which blocked you from calling cell phones. Brandy was from the 'hood, and had a father, brother, cousin, and a baby daddy who were all incarcerated, so she sympathized with Mike. Plus she'd had a crush on him since back in the day, so she went ahead and let him use the phone.

"Look here, they should be lettin' Nikki go in a hot minute. So get her mama to scoop her, then give her the paper for my bond so I can get the fuck up out this bitch befo' the weekend over."

"How much yo' bond is?"

"Hundred and fifty stacks."

"A hundred and fifty thousand?!! Goddamn, what the fuck they got yo' ass charged wit'?" asked Ant D.

"Just some bullshit from that chase, and some other shit they talkin' 'bout they found in the spot. Nigga, you know these crackers be jackin' bonds up high as a muh'fucka so they greedy asses can get a cut, and put they sorry ass kids through college. But you already know what it is. Ten percent get a nigga out. So make it do what it do."

Brandy started motioning for Mike to wrap it up. The next shift would be coming on in a few minutes, and she wasn't trying to get written up... not even for Mike. "Look, nigga, I gotta go."

"Don't even stress that shit, my nigga. I got you! And as soon as you touch down, we goin' to see Meka and find out who them fuck niggas was that fucked her up. After that... you already know what it is."

"Yeah I know, I know. Let me get my ass off this phone tho', 'cause it look like B finna have a goddamn seizure," Mike laughed.

"Ok, bet. Don't drop the soap, muh'fucka," Ant joked.

"Nigga, fuck you!" retorted Mike, and he handed the phone back to Brandy. "Good lookin' out, B, fa' real."

"Ain't no problem, Mike. If you need anything else when I'm on duty, anything at all, just holla' at me," stated Brandy, with a look of lust on her face that didn't attempt to conceal the meaning behind her words.

Mike knew exactly what the business was, but he had bigger, more important shit on his mind. So he just said, "I'ma get at you, baby."

Chapter 25

After the intake process, Mike was thrown into the large holding tank with about twenty other individuals. They were all waiting to be assigned to a block in the "old jail", which was where most of the inmates with more violent charges were kept, or a pod in the "new jail." As usual, the holding cell was packed with mostly Black men, waiting to be sent to their assigned housing units. Individuals charged with everything from murder, to something as simple as public drunkenness. Crackheads, winos, rapists, dope boys, and junkies going through withdrawal all in the same spot at the same time.

Mike looked around the cell to see if he saw any familiar faces - friend or foe. He recognized a few niggas he had seen here and there around town, but nobody he really fucked with like that. They gave him a few nods of acknowledgement, and he did the same in return. After assessing the niggas in the cell with him and not detecting any real threat, Mike began to make his way over to the filthy toilet that a heroin addict had just finished throwing up in so he could take a piss.

That's when he spotted him... A pussy ass nigga he had robbed a few months back named Turk was sitting on the cement slab against the wall. Turk was a wanna-be pretty boy nigga from out of town that wore a lot of fake Gucci, Louis Vuitton, and Prada. It was rumored that Turk liked the boys just as much as the girls. He was the type of clown ass nigga that had a habit of bragging about how many bitches he was fucking, and how much paper he was stacking. This made him a prime target to get his dumb ass robbed.

He had tried to play the tough guy role but that pistol in his face made him bitch up and started crying. He literally begged Mike to let him keep his worthless life. Feeling sorry for him, he just took the couple thousand dollars he had on him and his jewelry, which had turned out to be fake. Then Mike had made him strip butt ass naked and run down the road in front of the whole projects, where he was supposed to have been getting money.

Now, as Mike bopped his way over to the toilet, he could feel Kirk staring at him as if he actually wanted to try him or something! Mike stopped, and immediately addressed the situation. "Nigga, you keep lookin' at me like somethin' wrong wit' yo' muh'fuckin' face, or somethin'. There a problem, nigga?!"

The entire holding tank got quiet, and the tension was thick enough to cut with a knife. Everybody waited for Turk to respond.

"Nah, son, everything good," said Turk unconvincingly.

"Nigga, you know yo' pussy ass ain't even built like that, so I'd advise you to stop lookin' all mean, like you done killed somethin'!"

In his heart, Turk was a straight coward. He really didn't want any problems with Mike, or anybody else for that matter. But at the same time, he couldn't just let Mike talk to him any kind of way in front of the rest of those niggas, so he stood up as if he was going to confront Mike.

As soon as he got to his feet, Mike started hitting him with a flurry of lightning quick punches to the face. At first Turk tried to fight back, but the ferocity of Mike's attack overwhelmed him. After a hard right to his chin, Turk dropped to the ground and balled up in the fetal position, covering his face as Mike kicked and stomped his ass into the cement. "Nigga, I'll kill yo' pussy ass!"

Turk whimpered and screamed for the guards at the top of his lungs. The rest of the holding tank just stood back and watched. It was a pitiful sight.

Suddenly the door to the holding cell swung open, and in rushed five heavily padded guards with an electric shock shield and restraints. In seconds, they had Mike on the ground, and in handcuffs and shackles. Two of the guards grabbed him by his shackles, and dragged him out of the cell. Once out of the cell, they picked him up and transported him to the S.H.U. (Special Housing Unit). There, they commenced to choking and beating him before throwing him into a 5'x7' cell with no windows. There was nothing in there to look at but concrete walls. At least it was clean though, thought Mike.

The S.H.U. was in the new jail, which had just recently been built, so it still had the scent of freshly painted walls in the air. But a cell was still a cell, and those particular ones had been designed to break down the most violent violators of the jail's rules and regulations. A psychologist made her rounds on a daily basis because so many had cracked under the pressure of the S.H.U. and attempted suicide. A few had succeeded.

It was a common occurrence for one to go to sleep, and wake up with the stench of someone else's feces in the air because that particular individual had smeared shit all over themselves, and their walls. Since all the ventilation was connected, a man could often find himself holding his breath as he tried to get his food down. That was no place for the weak.

"Yo' nigga, what's up" somebody yelled through the vent from the cell to Mike's left.

"Ain't shit… who 'dat?" asked Mike. The voice sounded familiar, but it was a little distorted coming through the air vent. There was no telling who it was.

"Nigga, this Monster. What's good, homey?"

Monster's real name was Christopher Wilkins. Back in the day when Chris was younger, the kids used to pick on him and call him Eddie Munster because he had a unibrow like the television character. But as Chris got older, and his crimes became more savage and brutal, everybody dropped the Eddie, and the Munster turned into

Monster. He'd been convicted of everything from manslaughter, to assault and battery with the intent to kill, to distribution of crack cocaine to a minor. His rap sheet read like a short story. But somehow he always seemed to catch a skid bid, and be right back out on the street within a matter of a few years. The word on the street was that the nigga was telling, but nobody knew for sure. It really didn't matter this time though. After all the publicity his last crime had received, the only way he'd be seeing the streets again anytime soon was if he could tell them where Bin Laden was.

A few months back, one of Chris' kids had come up missing. The boy was named Trevarus, and he was only five years old at the time. The local authorities had immediately issued an Amber Alert. Once the news media picked up the story, there were people, White and Black, coming from all over the Upstate to help the police and rescue teams search for the young boy. For days on end, they went out searching everywhere for signs of Trevarus, but never found him. Finally, after a full week of searching the Greenline community where he'd gone missing, Chris had led the police deep into the woods behind his house to a spot where there was a fresh mound of dirt between two trees.

"He's down there," was all Chris said. The cops dug the body of five year old Trevarus Wilkins out of his makeshift grave. Due to the unseasonably hot weather, the state of his decomposition had advanced to the point where you could smell his remains, even through the black trash bag he'd been thrown into.

Monster claimed the whole thing had been a mistake. He said he'd been giving his son a bath, when he had accidentally bumped his head and died. Monster said that he panicked because of his record, and had placed his son into a Hefty trash bag and buried him in the woods behind the house. An autopsy of the young child's body revealed otherwise. Trevarus had bruises, not only on his head, but also on several other places on his little body that showed a pattern of abuse. Monster was charged with first degree murder, and was being held without bond. Due to the crime being so high profile, he was immediately placed in S.H.U.

"Ain't shit good, muh'fucka!" Mike responded, after he realized who he was talking to. After growing up in the system without ever even getting the chance to meet his parents, it was hard for Mike to understand how somebody could kill their own flesh and blood like that. Their own son. That was like killing a part of yourself.

He wished he could spit on that nigga and lay hands on him. Mike told that muh'fucka how he felt. "Nigga, yo' pussy ass *should'a* killed yo'self! If we ever go out on the rec yard together, I'ma show you who the real monster is, nigga!"

"Aww nigga, you just talkin'" said Monster, like he was cucumber cool. That dude was a mess. He was unaffected by anyone's opinion of him about that shit. He was what you called pure evil. The nigga had no soul.

Mike said, "I ain't got shit else to say to yo' bitch ass! I'ma show you better than I can tell you. Sick ass muh'fucka!"

$$$

A couple of days later, Mike sat on the hard steel bed in his cell trying to eat his lunch through the putrid stench of shit. Some clown up the hall had smeared it all over himself and his walls, probably to protest something, if that made any sense. The smell was suffocating him, so Mike gave up trying to eat and threw his tray against the wall in frustration and anger.

That damn S.H.U. was beginning to get to him. He got up off the bed and walked over to the stainless steel toilet to take a piss. As he began to urinate he felt an intense burning sensation, so he yelled out in pain. It felt like fire was coming from the head of his dick! He looked closer, and noticed a yellow, pus-like discharge coming from the tip. Mike sat back down on the steel bed, and contemplated who could have burned him. He had been fucking with a few different girls before he got with Nikki, so he wasn't even really sure.

Mike thought about the orgy he and Ant had with those strippers. That was probably when it happened. He just hoped he hadn't passed anything on to Nikki. There was no telling how she would take something like that. He couldn't even tell her. Mike stared at the wall, depressed about his situation.

A voice came blaring out over the intercom in his cell, interrupting his pity party. "*Smith, pack your shit! Your ass is gettin' out!*"

"About goddamn time!" Mike exclaimed. The first thing he had to do when he got out was see a doctor. He needed a shot of penicillin, or something. Fast!

Chapter 26

Days after she'd awakened from her coma, Ant D finally walked through the doors of Meka's hospital room in the intensive care unit to see about her. His sister was sitting up in bed with a bowl of soup on a tray in front of her. Meka and Glo were in the middle of a conversation about something, but Ant cut it short. He walked over to his sister and gave her a hug that lasted a lot longer than they would've normally embraced. No words were spoken, and none were needed. Neither Meka nor her brother was the type to openly display their affection, so that hug said a lot more than words could've expressed.

Despite the fact that they were fraternal twins, Ant D and Meka shared a love for one another that was a lot deeper and more intense than anyone, including Gloria and Mike, could ever fathom. They were brother and sister, but they were also lovers, and had been for years now. Their relationship was both simple and extremely complex. After so many years of being on their own, and depending on one another for emotional support, their relationship had developed into a love beyond the kind most brothers and sisters shared.

Meka and Ant wouldn't hesitate to die, or kill for one another. But that was something that never needed to be said out loud. After all the shit they'd been through it really wasn't necessary. They both knew what time it was.

"Damn nigga, you tryna put me back in a coma," joked Meka,

as she let her brother go. "Let me find out you done got all soft on me."

"I never thought I'd say this, but damn it feels good to hear yo' slick ass mouth," said Ant D, smiling. "The doctor said you might end up retarded, but I told him you was already a lil' slow, so we was used to that by now."

"Nigga, fuck you!" said Meka, laughing. They joked and tripped with each other for a few more minutes, until finally Meka said, "Mama, I need to holla' at Ant for a minute."

Gloria wasn't stupid. She caught the meaning behind her daughter's request. She said, "Sure baby," and stepped out of the room to give her children some privacy.

"Where Mike at?" asked Meka.

"The police had trapped that nigga off a few days ago for some bullshit, but we bonded him out this morning. So his ass should be here any minute. That's why I'm just now comin' through. Mama told me how you wanted to see both of us, so I wanted to make sure he was out before I came. Meka, what the fuck happened? Who did this shit?"

Before she could respond, Mike came through the door and flashed his $40,000 smile. He walked over to Meka and gave her a brief hug, and kissed her on the forehead. "What's the verdict, baby girl, how you feelin'?"

"Like shit. What about you? I heard they had yo' ass locked up."

"A lil' light somethin'. Wasn't nothin' too heavy. I'm good though. Just happy to see yo' ass is still alive," Mike said, and lit up the other half of the blunt he was smoking on the way over.

He passed the el to Meka, and said, "You want some of this?"

She shook her head and said, "Naw, I'm good."

After a couple of deep pulls, Mike passed the blunt to Ant D. "Meka, do you remember what happened to you?" he asked, with weed smoke coming out of his nostrils. "We put the word out on the street that we had a hundred stacks for any info on what went down, but we ain't never hear shit. If you remember, you need to let us know what time it is, so we can handle that shit. 'Cause whoever them niggas is, they livin' on borrowed time, ya' heard?"

Meka had known Mike long enough to know that he didn't make threats without being 100% willing to carry them out. So she knew that once she told him and her brother the events that had led up to her being laid up in that hospital bed, there was no turning back. And that was exactly what she wanted.

Meka took a deep breath, and then proceeded to tell her story. "Y'all remember that nigga named Rico, right?"

Mike and Ant both nodded their heads, so she continued. "Well I ain't never told y'all, but the night that shit went down with Twan, him and that dusty ass bitch from Fieldcrest, Tasha, saw us eatin' at the Red Dragon together. So in other words, I was the last person Twan was seen with."

"I never really thought about it again until Labor Day weekend. I had just finished getting my hair and nails done at Sylvia's, and was walkin' to my truck when outta nowhere, a nigga came up behind me and started chokin' me out. I fought wit' the nigga, and tried to get free 'cause I remembered that .25 you had gave me was in my purse, Ant. I started to reach for it, but before I could get it out, another nigga who had been in the cut, came over and punched me in the stomach. I was like "oh shit!" That nigga knocked the wind outta me."

Meka paused, and shook her head. "I blacked out, and when I came back to, they had me in some house strapped to a bed, with nothin' on but my panties and bra. All of them had masks on, but one of the voices sounded familiar. Anyway, when I told them pussy muh'fuckas I wasn't finna answer no questions, one of the niggas got mad and punched me in the mouth. So I spit in his face."

Ant D and Mike exchanged little smiles, neither surprised by Meka's last sentence. That was her all day.

She kept on. "After that, the nigga went off and started beatin' the shit outta me. I couldn't do anything but lay there and take it. After he finished gettin' off, the other two clowns that were there with him started gettin' scared, talkin' 'bout how some nigga named Zulu ain't want no bodies poppin' up."

"Zulu? I heard that nigga 'posed to be supplyin' half the fuckin' south!" stated Ant D.

"Yeah, well come to find out, the nigga Zulu was Twan's uncle."

"You bullshittin'," said Mike in amazement. "How the fuck you was wit' that nigga all that time, and ain't know his uncle was the biggest supplier in the fuckin' southeast? Shit, if we would'a known that, we could'a hit *his* ass instead of Twan."

"Damn right," Ant D chimed in. He and Mike young and brave.

"Twan ain't never told me shit about what he did, or who he did it wit'. He used to always say he wanted to keep that part of his life away from me. Shit, I never even met that nigga's mama. Anyway, them niggas kept yappin'. They either thought I was unconscious, or figured that when they killed me I wouldn't be able to talk anyway, because they started talkin' real reckless."

"So this what it is. This nigga Zulu tryna find out who killed Twan 'cause Twan was his sister's youngest son, and he started him in the game. I guess Rico remembered seeing us at the Chinese place that night, and put two and two together. But he wasn't really sure, that's why he snatched me up. Them other two clowns was just going along wit' it."

"You ain't never hear them say they names," asked Mike.

"Yeah, one of 'em is named Ty. The other one they called Black, or some shit. So anyway, like I said, after Rico finished beatin' me up they got scared. Rico told them all they had to do was get rid of my body, and they'd be straight. He said that he already had it figured out, but before they got rid of me they might as well have a little fun. That's when they took turns raping me."

Meka stated this as matter of factly as a person would say it's hot outside on a summer day. It wasn't that the rape didn't affect her. It really did, but she refused to be a helpless victim. Those bastards weren't going to ruin her life. She couldn't be breaking down, crying and shit. She didn't do that. *"Naw, that ain't me,"* she thought.

"After they raped me, they took turns pissin' on my face, and all types of other crazy shit. I don't really know what happened after that because I blacked out. The next thing I remember is wakin' up and seeing mama over there in that chair."

The silence that followed was louder than thunder. Mike and Ant were both stunned and speechless. They had to let what Meka had just told them sink in. Damn, she had been through a lot. The weed they smoked had the description of her ordeal playing in their minds as vividly as a high definition movie. Images of her being raped and pissed on had their blood boiling.

Ant D was the first to break the silence. "Meka, you ain't even gotta say no mo'. Them niggas is dead!!"

"I just want y'all to do one thing for me," said Meka.

"What's that?"

"Get Rico, but whatever you do, please don't kill him. Save him for me. Rico's mine." She nodded her head slowly.

"If that's what you want, then that's what it is," stated Mike. He and Ant talked to Meka for a few more minutes, and then they left her room so she could get some rest.

About five minutes after their departure, Detective Daniel Patterson walked through the door. The strong scent of marijuana smoke still lingered in the air. The detective noticed it, and wondered what nigger had the heart to do something as dumb as smoke reefer in a hospital room in I.C.U. He decided against commenting, to avoid putting Meka on defense. He had come there for answers.

He gave Meka a fake smile, and said, "Tameka, my name is Detective Patterson. How are you feelin'?" His voice belied the fact that he could care less about her well being.

"I've been better."

"Well I just need to ask you a few questions." He wasn't asking her permission, he was telling her.

Seeing that he wasn't going to leave, Meka agreed. But she hoped he would be quick. She wanted that cracker to hurry up and ask his questions, and get the fuck on. She was ready to go back to sleep.

He cleared his throat, and said, "Tameka I'm investigating what happened to you several weeks ago. I need to know if you remember anything that might help me bring these animals in."

Meka just thought for a second. She also wanted the perpetrators brought to justice. The difference was that she had no belief or trust in the American criminal justice system. She'd seen rapists and child molesters go free, and drug dealers who'd been selling hand to hand get locked up for the rest of their lives. So the only justice that she had faith in was the court niggas held in the streets, with hot slugs and death as the sentences. Not in some racist cracker's courtroom with a judge who didn't really give a fuck one way or the other.

Finally, she said, "Detective Patterson, to tell you the truth, I really don't remember anything that happened to me. You know, the doctors say that amnesia is pretty common in cases like mine."

Twenty-plus years of experience on the force told Daniel Patterson that the little Black whore in front of him was lying through the few teeth she had left. For what reason, he didn't know, but he definitely intended to find out. Hopefully he'd get things wrapped up soon, and get the publicity and promotion he'd been chasing all those years. After that, those fucking coons could kill themselves all they wanted.

Chapter 27

It was Halloween, 2006. October 31st. Some people called this nationally celebrated holiday the devil's night…and for good reason. It was a well documented fact that throughout the United States, more crimes were committed on Halloween night than on any other night of the year. And that Halloween wasn't going to be any different. In fact, in Greenville, SC the crime rate would get worse that year.

$$$

Sweaty, out of breath, and completely naked, Ty lay back on the bed and watched a young, brown skinned stallion mount his hard dick reverse cowgirl style. With her back to him, she began to slowly rock back and forth. The girl was only twelve years old, but had a body a full grown woman would envy. Her breasts were perky little C-cups with dime sized nipples that were rock hard. Her stomach was completely flat with a faint line of pubic hair on it, which ran from her belly button all the way down to the curly mass between her legs. She had no waist to speak of, which made her ass appear even larger than it was. Her thighs were thick, and her feet were small and sexy. The irony of it all was the fact that she had a face so young and innocent, a person who didn't know her would've sworn she was still a virgin.

Ty was twelve years older than the girl, and needless to say, a lot more experienced when it came to the streets. His swagger, and the fact that he was stacking a little paper had lots of the younger girls over in West G-Ville, where he was hustling, infatuated with him. So when he had asked Shay to come to his spot on Perry Ave. to chill, she had readily and eagerly agreed.

Tired of fucking with immature, broke ass niggas her own age, she was more than willing to be with Ty. And do any and everything he asked. Young and naïve, and like so many other girls who grow up without a father figure around to guide them, Shay believed that her willingness to please a man sexually would make him fall in love with her. But in reality, she would just be another young freak that Ty would add to a long list of bitches he'd fucked.

Shay started bouncing on Ty's dick, going faster and faster, until beads of sweat formed on her forehead. She closed her eyes and rode him, while simultaneously using her thumb and index fingers to pinch her hard, sensitive nipples.

While Shay rode his cock, Ty admired her firm, young, round ass as it went up and down. He loved the way her butt cheeks jiggled when she came back down on him. Ty rubbed two fingers on his right hand down Shay's sweaty ass crack. He then brought those fingers up to his nose and inhaled her musty scent. After that, he licked both fingers clean.

Ty was a straight freak, and he loved turning young girls out. He placed his hand on Shay's back and pushed her slightly forward. Now her ass cheeks spread open while she rode him, exposing her tight little asshole. Ty got excited just at the thought. He loved that "brown eye." He spit on his middle finger and slowly inserted it into Shay's asshole.

Shay tensed up at first. She wasn't a virgin, but she'd never had anyone stick their finger up her ass like that. But the more Ty plunged his finger in her ass, the more she liked it. The sensation it gave her body threw her into a frenzy. She began to go crazy on Ty's dick, bouncing and rocking faster and faster, until her whole body was covered in sweat. Her tight pussy was sopping wet, and her juices drenched Ty's balls, along with the sheets underneath them. Unable to hold back any longer, he closed his eyes and curled his toes. He groaned, and got ready to bust his nut up in Shay.

Suddenly, there was a loud ass *BOOM* from the front of the house. It sounded like somebody had just blown the front door off its hinges with a bomb, or some shit. The noise pushed Ty over the edge, and he began to involuntarily skeet wildly inside of Shay's hot, young, box. While he was releasing hot semen in her, two masked men entered the bedroom dressed in all black. One was wearing a Michael Myers, the killer from the movie "Halloween", mask. The other one was wearing the infamous Jason Vorhees hockey mask from the movie "Friday the 13th."

Ty opened his eyes and looked at the two figures standing by his bed. They each had large guns in their hands. He wished it was just a joke, but he knew that shit was for real.

Shay started screaming at the top of her lungs, so the one wearing the Michael Myers mask quickly pressed his black Glock 9mm to her sweaty temple. "Shut the fuck up," he calmly ordered.

Shay fell silent immediately, and he continued. "You got thirty seconds to get yo' shit, and get the fuck up outta here."

She didn't doubt that he would kill her so she took heed to the warning. Fearfully, she hopped off of Ty's limp dick, and quickly grabbed her belongings while the gunman in the Jason mask counted down the seconds. "10, 9, 8, 7…" She didn't even bother to put her shoes on. Shay ran out of the house, too frightened to even look back.

Paralyzed with fear, Ty just lay there on the bed unable to move or speak. He had a silly ass expression on his face. He looked like "*what the fuck?*"

The one wearing the Jason mask slowly lifted his sawed off twelve gage shotgun until it was in Ty's face. Ty stared into the double barrels, and all he saw was darkness that seemed to stretch on for infinity. He realized he had met his demise.

"Trick or treat, muh'fucka!!" ***BOOM!!*** Blood and brain matter splattered all over the walls and bed. What used to be Ty's face was now nothing more than a gaping hole of blood and flesh. His skull was obliterated from the force of the blast, which made it possible to see damn near all the way through his entire head.

The gunman in the hockey mask laughed, and said, "I think I can see this nigga last thoughts before he died." Ant, A.K.A. Jason Voorhees, laughed again.

"Yeah, he was thinkin' *OH SHIT*! And he was 'bout to shit on his self too!" said Mike, laughing. Befittingly, he was Mike Myers. He lifted the 9mm in his hand and took aim at Ty's already lifeless body. He mercilessly emptied more slugs into his partially headless torso. Once the clip was on "E", the two menacing figures turned and fled from the house. They bailed on Ty's mangled corpse, and disappeared into the moonlit night.

$$$

Later on that night, it was Black's turn. Deeply engrossed in a dice game, he wasn't even expecting the heat that was coming.

"Eight'll get me ten! Eight bring ten, muh'fuckas! Y'all know what time it is. Get right or catch flight, niggas," exclaimed the short dark skinned man, as he shook the dice in his right hand. After shaking them for a few seconds, he brought his cupped hand up to his mouth and blew on the dice for good luck. Afterwards, he dropped them and let them roll on the ground against the wall. One of the dice showed a six, and the other a three. It wasn't Black's point but he didn't crap out either, so he picked the dice back up, and the side bets increased.

There were only five dudes directly involved in the game with actual money on the line. But just like at any other dice game, there were five or six other niggas just chilling on the sidelines watching the action. They were drinking and smoking trees, and talking trash just to hype shit up. The dice game had been going on for a little over an hour. During that time, the pot had grown to over $10,000 cash money. The bread was piled up on the ground in an assortment of bills, so they were a prime target for some thirsty goons. But just about everybody out there was strapped.

As Black prepared to roll again, the other men made more side bets on whether or not he'd hit his point. Some bet on what the next number was going to be. Despite the cool weather, Black was sweating profusely. He shook the dice, and started talking that shit again.

"Eight bring ten, nigga! Get ya' mind right, bitches! Eight bring ten, nigga!" Black was talking shit, but he was secretly saying a prayer to Jesus, Jehova, Allah, Yahweh, God, and any other higher power he could think of while he attempted to roll his eight. He couldn't afford to crap out. If he did, he wouldn't be able to pay the dude that had fronted him some work earlier that week. He wouldn't be able to pay for his consignment, nor would he be able to re-up. If he crapped out, he was dead in the game - literally. So it was more than just a game to Black. It was so serious.

But if he did fuck around and hit a seven or roll snake eyes, he figured he could always pull out the chrome .357 he had hidden in his waistband, and rob those niggas. Black really hoped it wouldn't come to that. He blew on the dice and rolled them against the wall... and he hit!

"What I tell y'all niggas, huh?! What I tell you muh'fuckas, huh?!" Black shouted, relieved and excited at the same time. "Eight get me ten," he yelled, as he bent down to pick up the 10 G's he'd just won.

"Yo, Black!" somebody yelled from behind the crowd. Black turned around, and so did everybody else. What they saw made them all start reaching for their pistols. Black went for the chrome .357 magnum conveniently tucked in his waistband. Before he could get it out, two figures dressed in black and rocking horror film masks ran up on the crowd firing indiscriminately from an AK-47 and an AR-15 assault rifle.

The rapid fire explosions from the barrels of the assault rifles lit up the night, and niggas scattered like roaches when the lights came on. A few tried to be brave and bust back, but their handguns were no match for those assault rifles' firepower. Through the hail of gunfire, a couple of dudes managed to get off a few wild shots, but the choppers easily turned their bodies into mangled pieces of flesh.

Black saw the carnage taking place around him and decided to run for his life. He and a few others were fortunate enough to get away before being gunned down.

Ant chased after them with the chopper but they split up and eluded him. He cursed under his breath, "Damn!" That nigga Black had gotten away. Ant trotted back to the spot where the crap game had been going on.

Mike was still over there. He had stayed behind to collect the bloodstained cash that had been dropped in the midst of all the confusion. He and Ant D put a few rounds into each of the fallen men's heads and bodies to make sure they couldn't testify in any courtroom. Afterwards, they both took off for the crack car that was parked around the corner.

Once on the road, they both removed their masks. "You get that nigga Black?" inquired Mike.

"Naw, that fuck nigga got away," Ant spat. From the look on his face, you could tell he was pretty disgusted.

"Fuck it, we'll get 'im. We'll get 'im. The nigga can run, but he can't hide."

Chapter 28

Over the next few days, Ant D and Mike rode around Greenville searching for Rico in a beat up, old, tinted out Chevy Nova they had gotten from this crackhead nigga named Mitch. Mitch was an old school smoker, but the young niggas in the 'hood still had love for him because he was a straight fool. He kept everybody laughing, despite their desperate and desolate living conditions. And when anybody needed a car real quick to do some dirt in, they got at Mitch. All he wanted was for dudes to look out for him with a nice piece of hard.

Ant D and Mike drove to every single spot Rico was known to frequent. They were looking for him, or anybody who had seen him recently. But they found neither. After hearing about what had happened to Ty, and how Black had barely escaped death himself, Rico knew that he was involved in whatever the fuck was going on. He had no idea Meka was still alive, so he assumed it had something to do with them killing her.

Rico wasn't sure, but he felt that shit in his gut. So he figured his best move would be to disappear for a minute, until he found out exactly what the fuck was going down, and who was behind it. Until then he was extremely vulnerable because he had no idea who was coming for him. Anybody could just walk up to him out of the blue, and blow his fucking head off. So Rico laid in the cut like a germ at a woman's house he fucked with in Anderson, SC.

After looking for that nigga for days on end and coming up with nothing, Mike told Ant D he had a plan that would bring Rico's bitch ass out of hiding.

After he listened to what Mike had in mind, Ant smiled, and said, "That's what it is. Let's do it!"

$$$

On a cool night in mid-November, Ant D pulled up to a house in West Greenville. The house was down the street from St. Francis Hospital, where Mike was born. Ant killed the ignition on the old Chevy Nova, and turned to Mike who was sitting calmly in the passenger seat. He asked, "You ready?"

"Yeah, but just stick to the script. We ain't tryna kill this old bitch, ya' heard?"

"I know what it is, nigga, let's go." Before they got out of the car, Ant pulled out a plastic baggy filled with coke. He rolled up a crisp twenty dollar bill, and took a long snort up each nostril.

"Goddamn Ant, you gettin' outta control wit' that shit, my nigga. You need to slow yo' ass down, homey, fa' real."

"Look, nigga, I got this here. I just fuck wit' this shit every now and then. Ain't nothin' serious, man. Trust me."

Mike knew he was lying out his ass, but that wasn't the time or the place to have that conversation. They had come to do some dirt, so he wanted to handle that shit, and get the fuck outta dodge. They could continue that conversation another time.

They got out of the car and sprinted up the short driveway to the front porch of a slightly rundown house. They were dressed in black again. Ant D knocked on the front door loudly. When they heard footsteps approaching the door, he and Mike pulled their ski masks down over their faces.

"Yes… who is it?" asked an older female voice from behind the door.

Without hesitation, both Ant and Mike backed up a few steps

and then charged the locked door. They used their shoulders to bust into the house, and knocked the woman backwards onto the floor.

Once inside the house, Mike quickly closed the door behind them. The Puerto Rican woman looked up in horror. She was still dazed from the impact of the door against her face, which had caused her nose to start bleeding profusely. At age 52, the woman was still very beautiful, and in relatively good health. But all of that was getting ready to change.

Without saying a word, Mike and Ant walked over to the woman and began beating the shit out of her with their closed fists, careful not to cause any fatal damage. Unable to do anything else, she balled up in the fetal position and silently prayed they would stop. I guess Jesus wasn't listening because they kept on beating her mercilessly, until they were tired.

Mike assessed the damage, and felt like they had accomplished their goal. He was prepared to leave, but that coke had Ant D in a zone. After he caught his breath, he started savagely stomping the woman, who lay prone on the floor defenseless.

"Chill out, homey, that's enough," said Mike. But Ant didn't hear him, or he wasn't listening, because he continued to stomp the woman into oblivion. After hearing something in the woman's body crack, Mike grabbed Ant, and said loudly, "Remember the plan, nigga! We ain't tryna kill this old bitch! If she's dead, she's useless!"

Knowing what he said was true, Ant stopped kicking the woman. Breathing heavily from the physical exertion, he said, "Yeah… you right. Let's get the fuck up outta here."

They turned and ran from the house back to the Nova. They jumped in the car and sped off down the street.

Sensing that her attackers had fled, the woman tried to get up and walk to the telephone, which was in the living room on the coffee table. Too weak to stand, she crawled on her hands and knees. When she finally reached the phone, she used her last little bit of strength to dial 911.

"911, what's your emergency?"

The woman tried to speak but no words came out of her mouth. Everything got dark, and she collapsed on the floor. The phone slipped from her grasp.

"Hello? 911, what's your emergency?" asked the operator again. When she didn't receive an answer, she felt like something was amiss. The operator dispatched a police car to the address that showed up on her screen.

Back in the Nova, Ant turned to Mike while he was driving, and said, "You think that shit's gonna work?"

"It should," Mike responded. "Ain't nothin' for certain 'cept death, but everybody got a weak spot. And it's usually somebody they love. Even the hardest niggas alive care about *somethin'*. All we gotta do now is sit back and wait for his pussy ass to pop up at the hospital."

Ant D turned his attention back to the road, and briefly reflected on the beating they had just given the older woman. Her name was Rosie Velasquez, and she was Rico's mother.

$$\$\$\$$$

The plan Mike had devised to bring Rico out of hiding went like clockwork. The next night, while sitting in the Nova in front of Memorial Hospital, he and Ant spotted Rico going inside. He was presumably going to visit his mother, who had been admitted the previous night with an assortment of injuries. Rosie Velasquez would live, but she had suffered numerous broken bones and other injuries as a result of the beating she'd taken.

"How you wanna do this shit," Ant asked Mike.

"As soon as he comes out, if ain't nobody else around, we snatch his ass up right in the parking lot. If there's people around, then we follow his ass and wait 'til he's alone. Knock his ass out, then throw him in the car."

"That's what it is then."

They waited for hours. They were beginning to grow impatient when finally out walked Rico. "There he go, there he go," Mike blurted out.

He and Ant D quickly got out of the car, and casually walked pass Rico like they were going into the hospital themselves. After letting him pass, they turned and followed him, staying a few feet behind so as not to attract his attention.

Once Rico got to his car, which was a cocaine white '83 Chevy Caprice, tinted and sitting on 24 inch chrome rims, Ant and Mike pulled their pistols out. They ran up on Rico quick, and he spun around and saw the guns in their hands. He tried to take off in the opposite direction, but he wasn't fast enough.

Ant used the butt of his chrome .45 to strike Rico in the back of his head. That caused him to lose his balance and stumble to the ground. He tried to get back up on his feet, but Ant gave him another blow to the back of his head. That one knocked him out cold, and left him unconscious on the parking lot pavement.

$$$

When Rico came to, he did so with a splitting headache. He also had two large, nasty gashes in the back of his head, where the butt of Ant's pistol had connected with his skull. But those were the least of his troubles. In minutes he'd wish that a bad headache was all he had to worry about. He tried to bring his hand up to his head, and realized that he was strapped to a bed, face down.

He abruptly opened his eyes and looked around the room, but he saw nothing in it. Except for the bed, the room was completely bare. He looked up at what appeared to be a window, and noticed that it was boarded up. He knew it was daytime because there were a few rays of light coming through the cracks, which gave the room an eerie glow.

Rico had no idea what time it was, or how long he'd been unconscious. *"Where the fuck am I?"* he thought, as the pounding in his head got worse. He jerked his arms and legs trying to free himself but it was useless. He was stuck. Finally, he realized he wasn't going anywhere, so he tried to remain as calm as possible.

"Hey Rico! I see you up," said somebody from behind him.

The voice gave Rico chills up his spine because the person who it belonged to was supposed to be dead. Rico looked around, but was unable to see the person who'd spoken.

"How you feelin', Rico? Are you comfortable?" asked the voice humorously.

Rico remained silent. The owner of the voice walked around to the side of the bed so he could see who was speaking to him. Rico looked at her face but couldn't believe his eyes. That had to be some kind of sick joke, or something. But he knew it wasn't.

After being discovered nearly dead in a dumpster, and then spending several weeks in a coma at Greenville Memorial Hospital, Meka had finally been discharged from the hospital on November 14th. That was just a day before Rico was kidnapped by Ant and Mike. The news of Meka's release had purposely been kept quiet. There was no party when she came home, or nothing like that. They had avoided celebrating just so they wouldn't fuck up their plan to kidnap Rico. Meka really wanted their reunion to be a special surprise.

The rehabilitation she had undergone when she came out of her coma had her almost completely back to normal. At least physically. And now that she was back on the street, revenge was the only thing she could think of. She'd been patiently waiting for that day for a minute now, so she intended to enjoy every second of it.

Meka looked at Rico and smiled, revealing the four solid gold teeth that replaced the ones he had knocked out weeks back. "Damn, Rico, I thought you'd be happy to see me. The last time we was wit' each other, we had so much fun together," Meka said sarcastically.

"Fuck you, bitch! I'ma kill yo' ass, you dick suckin' ass slut!" Rico had yet to realize the seriousness of the tight spot he was in.

"Awwwww. Rico, you already had yo' chance to do that, baby," said Meka in her sweetest voice. "Now I'ma show you how it's 'posed to be done." After that, she walked out of the room.

A few minutes later she returned, grinning. She said, "Now we're fixin' to have us a little fun. That is what you called it, ain't it, Rico?" she asked mockingly.

Meka began to undress. Rico strained his head and neck to see her, and wondered what that crazy ass bitch was up to. She turned her back to him and seductively wiggled her ass, slowly sliding her silk panties off. She bent over and let him get a good look at her pussy lips from behind.

When she turned back around, Meka was completely naked. Her body was still as beautiful as ever. In fact, the days of rehabilitation had her looking toned and tight. She bent over and retrieved something from under the bed. When she pulled the object out, the realization of what she intended to do hit Rico like a ton of bricks.

Meka slowly put on a 12 inch strap-on dildo and secured it around her waist. The plastic penis protruded out in front of her threateningly. When he saw that big black strap-on dick, Rico's eyes filled with fear. He tried to cop a plea. "L-l-look, Meka, d-don't do nothin' crazy, alright? L-l-let's talk about this shit. I got some bread saved up…"

Uninterested in anything he said, Meka picked up her panties from the floor and stuffed them in Rico's mouth. That silenced his pathetic pleas for mercy. She had no pity for that mothafucka. She undid his pants, and then snatched his jeans and boxers down so that his naked ass was exposed. Meka laughed cruelly, and slapped him on the backside hard as hell. "Damn, baby! You got a *nice* ass! I'm 'bout to tear this shit up!"

Meka saw the expression on Rico's face, and laughed. She kept on fucking with him, and treating him like a bitch. "I'ma wear your back out, and I want you to tell me you like it."

After that, she climbed onto the bed and positioned herself behind him. Without any further ado, she forcefully plunged the artificial penis in Rico's asshole without any form of lubrication whatsoever.

Her entry was rough and painful. Rico screamed as loud as he could. "Aaaarrrrrgghh!!!" But his cries of agony were muffled by the panties Meka had stuffed inside of his mouth.

Over the next 45 minutes, Meka violated Rico's manhood in every way imaginable. After she was through, he lay motionless on the bed in a pool of his own blood, piss, and shit. The mattress was also soaked with the endless tears he had shed, which were still rolling from the corners of his eyes as he lay there prone. The pain he'd experienced was so excruciating that he'd passed out several times during his horrible ordeal. Each time he woke up, he realized Meka wasn't finished with him. But the physical pain was nothing compared to the mental anguish and humiliation that he felt by being raped by a woman.

Rico lay there on the bed wishing for death. Meka stood up, still wearing the dildo. But it was now soiled with his feces and blood. She walked into the front room without a word. She returned seconds later with a black 9mm pistol.

Meka walked around where Rico could see her without straining. She wanted him to see her face. She placed the pistol to his temple and pulled the trigger, laughing as she ended his worthless life. She said, "See, Rico. Now *that's* how it's done. *That's* how you kill a muh'fucka!"

She fired again and put another slug in his head. Meka's ears rang from the loud gunfire, and the smell of cordite filled the air. She looked down at what remained of Rico's head, and was smugly satisfied. Revenge was indeed a dish best served cold.

Chapter 29

The large mansion was 15,000 square feet. It consisted of five bedrooms, four and a half bathrooms, a dining room, a den, and a personal home theater that seated 15 people. There was a huge patio out back, and a large swimming pool in the backyard, which was usually full of naked women. There was also a five car garage that held an assortment of expensive vehicles. Everything from an '06 china white Mercedes Benz S550 with chrome 20 inch rims, to an '06 black on black, fully equipped with TV's, DVD, and stereo system Cadillac Escalade sitting on 26 inch chrome Giovanni rims. Not to mention the old school 1976 Carolina blue Cadillac Deville with cream leather interior. And every one of the vehicles was equipped with bulletproof paneling and stash boxes. Needless to say, their owner thought ahead.

The prime real estate sat on some of the most beautiful land in the whole upstate of South Carolina. The grass was so lush, green, and perfectly maintained that it appeared artificial upon first sight. In front of the mansion there was a manmade cascading waterfall fountain, which further accentuated the landscape with an air of beauty and wealth. If that house was on MTV Cribs, it would've taken a two part special to feature it. If the property owner was an entertainer, or had legal sources of income, it definitely would've made the cut. But neither was the case.

The mansion had numerous hi-tech security equipment in

place. It started with a tall, black, iron fence that was manned by two heavily armed guards at the entrance. The guards were rotated on 8 hour shifts. There were motion sensitive security cameras strategically placed throughout the grounds, which automatically activated whenever they detected movement. The cameras would then broadcast on a closed circuit channel in the guard's station, and on several monitors throughout the house.

There were also two specially trained rottweilers named Bonnie and Clyde that roamed the estate. They were always ready to tear apart anyone who came upon the grounds unannounced, whose scent they were unfamiliar with.

At times all of the extra security measures were a hassle, but they were absolutely necessary. The owner of the 3.5 million dollar home was one of the most powerful, respected, feared, and hated men in the whole south. He was the founder and mastermind behind one of the most notorious criminal organizations the Carolina's had ever seen: M.B.M. M.B.M. stood for Money By any Means, an organization that ruled the southeast's narcotic trade with a fist of iron.

There was no room for competition. If any existed, they were systematically targeted for extermination and brutally murdered. This was done as an example to others to show them that there was only one crew in town. Fortunately, this only had to be done a few times in order for the local hustlers to catch on. Then they either joined the team and made money, got out the game, or died a violent, painful death.

People were always speculating as to how many soldiers were in M.B.M. but those that said didn't know, and those that knew didn't say. At least not if they valued their lives. M.B.M. was a close nit, tightly ran criminal enterprise that had a chain of command more akin to the Army. But its financial structure was that of a Fortune 500 company. Those two elements combined made it an extremely ruthless and profitable organization. The man behind it all was none other than the feared gangster and nefarious mastermind, Zulu.

$$$

Wearing a royal blue terrycloth robe, with an embroidered gold Z on the breast, Zulu sat and listened as Black told him his take of the events that had taken place over the past few weeks. Black was careful to leave out anything that would place him in a bad light.

Zulu sat there listening and slowly deliberating while eating his breakfast. As Black explained who was responsible for his nephew's death, his calm demeanor belied his murderous intentions. His manner unnerved Black.

"So you're telling me that this girl Meka, who used to be my nephew's girlfriend, had Twan set up to get robbed by her brother and another nigga named Mike? How do you know this? Where did you get this information?"

"Zulu, this what it is, man. I'm tellin' you!" said Black emphatically. "That shit is all in the streets, bruh. I'm tellin' you, dog! Meka was Twan's main girl, and she was the last one wit' him before that shit went down. Then all of a sudden, after he dead, her and them other niggas coppin' shit like they won the fuckin' lotto or somethin'! Now you got niggas sayin' fuck you, and gettin' they work from them fuckin' wet backs. They tryna open up shop, thinkin' shit a game 'round here!"

Zulu continued to eat his food while he absorbed the information he'd just been given. Finally, after he finished his meal and washed it down with a glass of freshly squeezed orange juice, he wiped his mouth with a linen napkin and tossed it on top of the remains of food on his plate. He looked Black fully in the eyes for the first time since he had arrived at his house. His glare was menacing and disturbing.

Black was unsure of what to do or say, so he did nothing. His heart began to race with fear, and his forehead broke out in beads of sweat. He just sat there fidgeting in his seat. He liked it a lot better when Zulu wasn't looking at him. A whole lot better. Quietly, with a ferocious intensity in his voice, Zulu said, "An example must be set. I want them to pay!"

Chapter 30

THE AFTERMATH

"I can't believe you would do this shit to me," screamed Nikki in the doctor's office. Nikki rarely, if ever, used profanity but she was absolutely livid. And not to mention completely embarrassed. During a routine monthly check up, she just found out she had contracted gonorrhea. And she was certain that it came from Mike because she hadn't been with anyone else sexually in months.

She started wildly swinging on Mike, who had come with her to see how their baby was doing. He grabbed her and placed his arms around her to prevent her from hitting him. She struggled to break free from his grasp but was unsuccessful.

"Nikki, listen. I'm sorry, baby. I'm so sorry. It was before I was wit' you though. I didn't even know until I was locked up in the county!"

"Then why didn't you tell me?! Huh? Why didn't you tell me?" Nikki asked, sobbing on Mike's shoulder. "Why did I have to find out like this? You're foul, Mike! I'm pregnant!"

Nikki never had an STD in her life. She wasn't even out there like that. At first she found it hard to believe the doctor's findings because she hadn't had any symptoms, but then she was informed that a woman could have an STD like gonorrhea for months and not know. But her doctor schooled her that it could turn into PID, or Pelvic Inflammatory Disease, which could be extremely painful and potentially dangerous, even more so for the baby she was carrying.

Mike felt like shit. "I don't even know why I ain't tell you, Nikki. I was stupid. And I guess I was too ashamed. But you gotta believe me when I tell you I ain't never cheated on you. *Never.*"

"Mike, I don't know what to believe right now." Nikki wanted to believe him. She really did, but there were so many thoughts running through her head she just didn't know what to do. How did she know he was telling the truth?

"Nikki, listen. We can work through this, baby. I know you mad right now, but we can work through this. I want you to be my wife." He released his hold on her and waited for a response.

Nikki drew back and slapped Mike with all the force she could muster. The blow to his face resounded loudly in the quiet confines of the doctor's office. Crying, she turned and ran out the door.

Over the next few weeks, Mike did everything in his power to win Nikki back. Flowers, candy, cards, phone calls. Whatever it took to win her trust back, and get her to come home. He'd never felt like this. Mike was far from a sucker. He had taken lives without blinking an eye, but being without Nikki actually had him physically sick. It was a pain he'd never known, and prayed he would never know again. He couldn't even eat.

Nikki was miserable without him as well, but she stuck to her guns because she was more hurt by the irresponsible way he'd handled her. How could he neglect to tell her about having an STD, especially when she was pregnant with his child? How dare he? She was frightened by the lack of consideration Mike had for her. She would've never done that to him. The notion that she'd given him her heart, and got back so little in return just didn't sit well with her. If he could do something that foul, he was capable of basically anything. He wasn't the man she thought she knew. Coming to terms with that was pretty sobering for the love hangover she had for Mike. She kept his ass on ice for weeks.

Mike was really going hard trying to redeem himself. He even bought Nikki a car, but she was totally unimpressed. Finally, he went for broke and put his words on paper, and then he mailed her the touching love letter he scribed.

Nikki was of a special breed. None of the jewelry and other materialistic shit he gave her moved her, but the humility of him writing that letter broke her. So she relented and took Mike back.

On the day of their reunion, they sat in Mike's living room and talked for hours about their relationship, and where it was going. Mike let Nikki know again that he wanted her to be his wife, and carry his last name. But this time he pulled out a five carat diamond ring and made it official.

Nikki beamed. She wanted to say yes so bad, but she gave him an ultimatum. "Mike… you know I love you, and I would love to be your wife. But only under one condition."

"What's that?"

"You've got to promise me that you're through with the streets. I can't take wondering if something is going to happen to you every time you go out, God forbid. Or fearing that the police are going to kick our door in at any given moment. I just can't live like that, baby."

Mike thought seriously about what Nikki was asking of him. The only life he'd ever known had been a life of crime. And honestly, he was afraid he wouldn't be able to make it in the legitimate world. He was an underworld type of cat. What would he do? He hadn't even finished high school. How would he provide for his new family?

Mike didn't know how he would do it just yet, but if it meant getting to keep Nikki and be a part of his child's life, then he was through. There would be no more thugging and street running. Just like that. Mike looked in her eyes and said it like he meant it. "Nikki, I love you. So okay, I'm out."

She smiled, and held out her hand. When Mike slid that rock on his future wife's ring finger, his chest swelled with pride. He and

Nikki were going to be a family. He really liked the sound of that.

$$\$\$\$$$

Mike couldn't have picked a better time to chill. The streets of Greenville were on fire. Over the past months, there had been a host of homicides, kidnappings, home invasions, and an assortment of other violent crimes that remained unsolved. The news media had started to take notice of the rise in violent crimes, and were making it seem as if The Sheriff's Department was either ill equipped to deal with the problem, or that they were just plain inadequate.

The President of the local branch of the NAACP, Ralph Flemming, had a different view of what was taking place in Greenville. When he was a guest on "60 Minutes" he was quoted as saying, "Mostly all of the victims of these unsolved crimes are young Black men and women. I find it very hard to believe that, if these same crimes were taking place in a predominately White neighborhood, they would remain unsolved for very long. This just goes to show how much a Black life is valued in this state. I guess ol' Jimmy Crow has just put on a suit and tie, and changed his name to James Crow."

Though Mr. Flemming had grown up in the Nicholtown section of Greenville, and cared about his people, he cared about his career even more. He was using all the media attention to advance his own goals, and launch a political career as a Democrat in a majority Republican state. That was just the type of publicity he needed to rally the people behind him and get some votes.

In order to refute the implications that The Greenville County Sheriff's Office was racist and indifferent to the crimes that remained unsolved, they issued this statement from a spokesperson:

"The Greenville County Sheriff's Office has never, under any circumstances taken race or nationality into consideration when investigating any crime. We are aware of the recent increase in crime, and have come up with a no-tolerance policy for any violators of the law. We have recently come up with an anti-crime task force, and they will be patrolling the streets on a more regular basis in an effort to curtail this recent rash of criminal activity. Also, we ask that anybody with any information that can help solve a crime dial 1-800-CrimeStoppers, or call the Sheriff's office. You can remain anonymous. And if your information leads to a conviction, then you will be rewarded. Thank you."

While Ralph Flemming and Greenville County were jockeying for position in the news and all the media attention, increased patrols were turning the city into a police state, making it damn near impossible for anybody involved in anything illicit to get money. So the 'hood was starving…

$$\$\$\$$$

"I'm tellin' you, Ant. I'm through, my nigga," Mike said seriously. "I can't afford to keep wildin' like we been doin', dog. All the shit we done did. All the shit we done got away wit', and we ain't dead, or lookin' at no serious time? I mean, I got them lil' charges I gotta deal wit', but a good hungry lawyer can eat that fuckin' case like they one a them starvin' Africans on them commercials. The ones wit' the flies all over their faces, and shit!"

"You through?! Through?!" asked Ant incredulously. "Nigga, what the fuck you been smokin' on? Fuck is you talkin' 'bout?"

"I'm talkin' 'bout gettin' out the game, nigga. I'm talkin' 'bout havin' a baby on the way that I wanna be around to be a father to. What nobody ever was to me. A *father*. I'm talkin' 'bout there's gotta be more to life than the shit we doin'! That's what the fuck I'm talkin' 'bout."

Ant scoffed, "Nigga, you on a trip wit' no map! Muh'fucka, the only thing more to this life is gettin' mo' money, gettin' mo' pussy, and getting mo' higher! After that, yo' ass die! Ain't no mo' to this life shit than that! Heaven ain't in no fuckin' sky! That shit right here on Earth, my nigga! Look at this money, nigga!"

Ant pulled out two large stacks of cash and flashed it at Mike. "You see this here? This here get you the flyest bitches, the flyest whips, and the freshest clothes to wear... So we in heaven right now, nigga!"

Ant laughed, and pulled out his personal coke stash. He rolled up a hundred dollar bill, and stuck it straight in the bag and took a generous snort. He loved indulging in his new habit. He was starting to live for it. He didn't even smoke anymore. He used to smoke copious amounts of exotic weed to get him high, but he had graduated to just fucking with that cocaine heavy. It was a more intense, surreal feeling. When he was high off it, he felt like he couldn't be touched.

"Ant's right, Mike," Meka chimed in. She'd been sitting on the couch in her mother's living room listening to the heated exchange between her brother and her "brother." "I can't see myself gettin' no regular 9 to 5, and slavin' for no muh'fuckin' cracker for the rest of my life for a salary that's barely gon' be enough to survive off of either. Coming home tired every night, livin' from check to check... that's for them suckas and squares, Mike, not *us*."

"Meka, you like a sister to me. Naw, fuck that, you *is* my sister. But I'm *out*." All Mike could think about was the new life growing inside Nikki's womb. That was his new beginning.

Ant D shook his head in disbelief, and took two more good snorts from his little bag of powder.

"Damn, Ant, slow that shit down!" said Meka. Over the past few weeks, she'd witnessed her brother's coke habit go from bad to worse.

Ant ignored his sister and addressed that lame shit Mike just said. "Fuck that! Nigga, I'ma get money 'til they put me six feet in the fuckin' ground! And it's gonna take an army of them muh'fuckas to take me out anyway, so that ain't happenin' no time soon! So *fuck* that nigga Zulu! And fuck the po-lice too! Fuck *all* them muh'fuckas! My name Ant D, nigga!" he stated animatedly, gesturing wildly with his hands.

Mike shook his head. His best friend was unbelievable. "Ant, look here, my nigga. I don't know what type of shit you on right now, but this ain't no Scarface movie, and you ain't Tony Montana! And even if you was, you see how that shit ended for him, right? This shit can't last, nigga!"

Ant got quiet for a second. He looked like he was deep in thought. He scratched his chin and said, "You know what, Mike... You right, I'm not Tony Montana..." With a screw face, he exclaimed, "I'm fuckin' *worse*!" After that, he beat on his chest three hard times.

Mike knew that was that coke talking, so any attempt to reason with Ant would be futile at the time. There was no use. Mike just shook his head. He said, "I'll get up wit' y'all later," and then he turned and broke out. After he walked out the front door, the screen door slammed shut behind him.

$$$

"Did you tell him?" asked Nikki.

"Yeah, I told him," responded Mike, with a hint of sadness in his voice. He felt bad for abandoning his old family. But at the same time, he felt a sense of relief at no longer having to look over his shoulder all the time. For the first time in his short life, he was actually happy. He looked at Nikki and her protruding belly, which not only carried a new life, but a new beginning. Now he had a chance to right his wrongs, and protect his child from the horrors he had faced growing up.

Nikki and Mike sat in his Escalade outside the entrance of an upscale eatery Downtown. They were talking and making plans for the baby, discussing the things they needed to get him. They had recently found out from a sonogram that the baby was going to be a boy. Upon hearing the news, Mike and Nikki were elated.

"What should we name him," asked Nikki, as they watched customers exiting from the restaurant that sunny winter day.

"What you mean what we gon' name him?" asked Mike jokingly. "He gon' be named after his daddy."

They both laughed. Nikki said, "Ok, you get this one, but the next one *I'm* naming." She laughed again.

Mike rubbed Nikki's stomach and felt his son kicking inside her womb. "You feel that?" he asked, with awe in his voice.

"Yeah, I feel him, baby. He's just like his daddy. Already fighting and starting trouble…"

All of a sudden a black '96 Chevy Impala came to a screeching halt beside the Escalade, facing the opposite direction. Before Mike could react, semi-automatic shots were fired from the front and rear windows. The barrage of gun fire was over within seconds, but the aftermath would last forever.

The Impala sped off, leaving the Escalade riddled with bullet holes. People slowly got up off the ground and started screaming for the police. There was blood everywhere, and shards of shattered glass all over the pavement. Folks were running and hollering, but there was no movement inside the vehicle.

In the distance, the blaring sound of ambulance sirens could be heard getting closer and closer. They were coming to hopefully save lives. But there was still no sign of life inside the Escalade…

The only thing ever constant in life is change. Some people change for the better, some change for the worse. But change is as inevitable as death. Unfortunately, sometimes change can come too little, and too late. Especially when you're willing to do… ANYTHING FOR PROFIT.

Coming Fall, 2010

Guns & Roses

Street Stories of Sex, Sin, and Survival

CAROLINE McGILL

Best selling Author of "A Dollar Outta Fifteen Cent"

GUNS & Roses

STREET STORIES OF SEX, SIN, AND SURVIVAL

In Stores Now!

Sex As A Weapon

A Caroline McGill Exclusive

CAROLINE McGill

Bestselling Author of "A DOLLAR OUTTA FIFTEEN CENT"

Sex
as a
WEAPON
THE GRUDGE

"A compelling and sinister tale of sex and suspense, this intriguing page-turner will change the way you think forever. Powerful message for all, this MUST-READ is classic!"

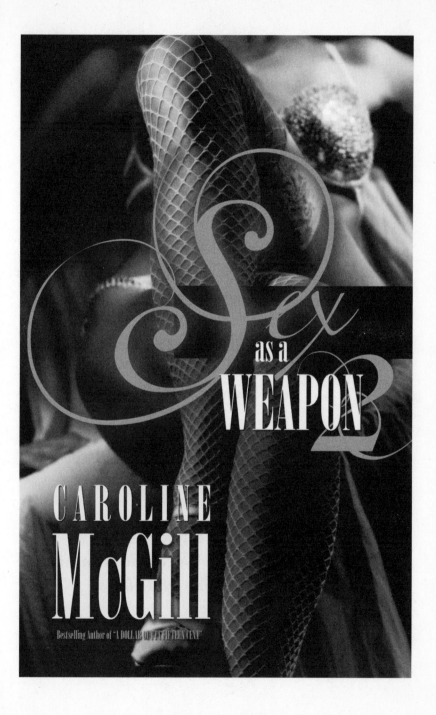

Sex
as a
WEAPON

CAROLINE
McGill

Bestselling Author of "A DOLLAR OUTTA FIFTEEN CENT"

Contact and Ordering Information

www.SynergyPublications.com

Synergy Publications
P.O. Box 210-987
Brooklyn, NY 11221

Phone: (718) 930-8818 • Fax: (718) 453-6760

Email the author at AmensTheTruth@hotmail.com
www.Facebook.com/Justin Amen Floyd
www.Twitter.com/JustinAmenFloyd

Order Form

Synergy Publications
P.O. Box 210-987 Brooklyn, NY 11221
www.SynergyPublications.com

_____ A Dollar Outta Fifteen Cent	$14.95
_____ A Dollar Outta Fifteen Cent II:	
Money Talks...Bullsh*t Walks	$14.95
_____ A Dollar Outta Fifteen Cent III: Mo' Money...Mo' Problems	$14.95
_____ A Dollar Outta Fifteen Cent IV:	
Money Makes the World Go 'Round	$14.95
_____ Sex As a Weapon: The Grudge	$14.95
_____ Sex As a Weapon 2	$14.95
_____ Guns & Roses (Vol. 1) Street Stories of Sex, Sin, and Survival	$14.95
_____ ANYTHING 4 PROFIT	$14.95
Shipping and Handling (plus $1 for each additional book)	$ 5.00
TOTAL (for one book)	$19.95
_____ TOTAL NUMBER OF BOOKS ORDERED	

Name (please print) :_____

First_____ Last_____

Reg. # (Applies if Incarcerated): _____

Address: _____

_____

City: _____ State: _____Zip Code:_____
Email: _____

*25% Discount for Orders Being Shipped Directly to Prisons
Prison Discount: ($11.21+ $4.00 s & h = $15.21)
**Special Discounts for Book Clubs with 4 or more members
***Discount for Bulk Orders - please call for info (718) 930-8818
WE ACCEPT MONEY ORDERS ONLY for all mail orders
Credit Cards can be used for orders made online
Allow 2 -3 weeks for delivery
Purchase online at www.SynergyPublications.com